C00 143

EDINBURGH CI

CW00857416

Ever Have One of Those Days?

A day when your teacher gives you a pop quiz? A day when your parents yell at you? A day when *everything's* going wrong?

That's the kind of day Jack's having. It's so bad, he wishes he were invisible.

Then Jack meets Luana. A girl who tells him she can *make* him invisible. All Jack has to do in return is one little favor.

Sounds easy, he thinks. I'll do it!

But on Fear Street, one *little* favor can turn into *big* problems for Jack!

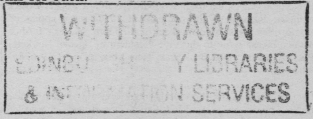
WITHDRAWN
EDINBU   Y LIBRARIES
& INF   TION SERVICES

Also from R.L. Stine

The Beast®
The Beast® 2

Available from MINSTREL Books

For orders other than by individual consumers, Pocket Books
grants a discount on the purchase of **10 or more** copies of
single titles for special markets or premium use. For further
details, please write to the Vice-President of Special Markets,
Pocket Books, 1633 Broadway, New York, NY 10019-6785,
8th Floor.

For information on how individual consumers can place
orders, please write to Mail Order Department, Simon &
Schuster Inc., 200 Old Tappan Road, Old Tappan, NJ 07675.

R·L·STINE'S
GHOSTS OF FEAR STREET ®

GRIMSBY CITY LIBRARIES

GO TO YOUR TOMB—
RIGHT NOW!

A Parachute Press Book

A
MINSTREL®
BOOK

Published by POCKET BOOKS
New York   London   Toronto   Sydney   Tokyo   Singapore

The sale of this book without its cover is unauthorized. If you purchased this book without a cover, you should be aware that it was reported to the publisher as "unsold and destroyed." Neither the author nor the publisher has received payment for the sale of this "stripped book."

This book is a work of fiction. Names, characters, places and incidents are products of the author's imagination or are used fictitiously. Any resemblance to actual events or locales or persons, living or dead, is entirely coincidental.

A MINSTREL PAPERBACK *Original*

A Minstrel Paperback published by
POCKET BOOKS, a division of Simon & Schuster Inc.
1230 Avenue of the Americas, New York, NY 10020

Copyright © 1997 by Parachute Press, Inc.

GO TO YOUR TOMB—RIGHT NOW! WRITTEN BY CAROLYN CRIMI

All rights reserved, including the right to reproduce this book or portions thereof in any form whatsoever. For information address Pocket Books, 1230 Avenue of the Americas, New York, NY 10020

ISBN: 0-671-00855-2

First Minstrel Books paperback printing November 1997

10 9 8 7 6 5 4 3 2 1

FEAR STREET is a registered trademark of Parachute Press, Inc.

A MINSTREL BOOK and colophon are registered trademarks of Simon & Schuster Inc.

Cover art by Mark Garro

Printed in the U.S.A.

EDINBURGH CITY LIBRARIES
LA3   C001433776?
CL
3.50 ASK 15/2/99

Want to hear about the absolute worst day in history? The kind of day that makes you want to disappear?

I wish it all happened to someone else. But it didn't. It happened to me.

It started at lunch. I should have known it was going to be a bad day when I saw that gray slab plop on my plate.

Meat loaf.

I was hoping for pizza or fried chicken—anything. Anything but meat loaf.

"All right! Meat loaf," my best friend, Connor, said from behind me. "My fave."

Connor eats everything and anything. It's sick.

I shook my head as I moved down the line. "I can't

believe you're excited about meat loaf. What planet are you from?"

Connor shrugged and brushed his long blond bangs out of his face. "The planet of hunger. It's lunchtime, and I'm starved."

No one would ever expect us to be best friends. Connor is a foot taller than any other kid in the seventh grade. I'm a foot shorter. He has straight blond hair. Mine is dark and curly.

Connor is a math whiz. I'm better at English. To Connor, everything has a logical explanation.

I don't agree. I think life is a lot more mysterious.

See, I live on Fear Street. I believe in things like vampires, ghosts, and monsters. Weird stuff happens on Fear Street. Supernatural stuff. I *know* people who have seen ghosts there. And worse.

So I take precautions. People tease me about it. But they haven't heard what I've heard.

I have a rabbit's foot key chain. And a fake silver bullet I bought in a junk shop. I don't think a werewolf would know it was fake. At least, I hope not.

And my lucky spider ring. That's the coolest of my lucky things. It's real silver, and the legs curl out around my finger. The eyes are shiny black stones. I've had it so long, I don't even remember where I got it.

As I picked up my lunch tray, I caught sight of my ring finger.

I should have known right then. I was definitely going to have a bad day.

I left my lucky spider ring at home.

I stared down at the meat loaf as I moved away from the lunch line. Thick brown goop dripped down it. I guess they call it gravy. It looked more like something my cat threw up.

I scanned the lunchroom for a good table. Way toward the back I saw two empty seats. I nodded toward them.

"Back there," I told Connor. "By the window."

I made my way toward the two empty seats but kept looking for a closer table. I stopped short when I saw one.

And this is where the trouble began.

Connor's tray slammed into my back. I jolted forward. My plate seemed to launch like a flying saucer. I watched in horror as it tumbled through the air in slow motion. Gravy splattered all over me.

The plate kept going. Straight at an unsuspecting target.

Mr. Lincoln.

He sat at the table right in front of me. His eyes widened in horror when he saw what was coming at him.

The plate landed—*splat!*—right in the middle of his shirt.

The meat loaf slid down to his lap.

Mr. Lincoln stood up and glared at me. Mashed potatoes stuck to his buttons. Brown, gloppy gravy dripped down his left sleeve. The meat loaf itself fell off his lap and onto the floor.

"I—I'm so sorry! Really, Mr. Lincoln," I stammered.

Mr. Lincoln's face was beet red. He looked as if he might explode. Without a word, he stormed out of the lunchroom.

Everyone around me was cracking up. I even heard Connor stifle a laugh. But he quickly bent down to help me pick up my plate and silverware.

Someone nearby started clapping. I glanced over to see who it was.

Oh, great. Frankie Todaro. Frankie struts around as if he's king of the school.

"What do you do for an encore, Meyers?" he called.

Everyone at Frankie's table laughed even harder. Even the girls. I didn't care so much about Penny Morris—she's annoying anyway, and we've been enemies since kindergarten.

But why did Brittany Carson have to be there?

Brittany has long brown hair and blue eyes. Sometimes I think she kind of likes me.

But right then the only thing I could think was—I wish I were invisible!

I slunk to the back of the lunchroom, where Connor waited for me. I plopped down in a chair across from him.

"Look at it this way, Jack. You don't have Mr. Lincoln until next year. By that time he'll have probably forgotten all about the meat loaf," Connor reasoned.

I gazed down at my plate and sighed. There was

4

only about a mouthful of mashed potatoes left on it. Even though I hated meat loaf, I was starving. So I went to get another helping.

Connor was done with his lunch by the time I got back to the table. He got up to dump his tray. I picked up my fork and took a stab at the meat loaf.

"Noooo, wait, don't eat me!" a strange voice shrieked.

I gasped and dropped my fork.

Was I hearing things? Did my meat loaf really talk to me?

I poked the gray slab with my finger.

"Stop that!" the voice bellowed.

My mouth dropped open. I glanced around, wondering if anyone else heard it. But no one else seemed to notice.

The voice continued. It sounded eerie, like an old, old woman. "I was once the lunch lady here. But they made me into a meat loaf. Don't eat me! Will you help me get revenge?"

I blinked in disbelief. How come no one else could hear this? Maybe this meat-loaf ghost had put a spell on them. Should I answer it?

Should I really answer a meat loaf?

"ANSWER ME!" the voice shrieked.

"Whoa!" I jolted backward, spooked.

Then a bright light flashed. I whipped around.

Mike Burger stood behind me with a Polaroid camera in his hands. His goofy brother Roy was laughing beside him.

"Got ya!" Mike cried.

If kids were graded on being bullies, Mike and Roy Burger would definitely get straight A's. They're both huge, and they love to tease the shorter kids in class.

Kids like me.

Connor walked back to the table. "What's going on?"

Everyone around started to crack up. Again.

I felt a tap on my shoulder. I turned around slowly.

It was Penny Morris. My worst nightmare.

She was holding a walkie-talkie. She pushed a button and spoke into it. "Jack, I am the ghost of the lunch lady, and I'm going to get yooooooooou!" she said in a creepy voice.

I heard her voice coming up from under my plate. I reached under the table.

Sure enough, I could feel something taped there. I yanked it free.

It was another walkie-talkie. Not a ghost.

Just a plain old walkie-talkie.

My face was burning up. I glared at Penny.

"I can't believe you actually fell for that, Jack," she said, sneering. "I mean, we all know you believe in ghosts and stuff but, come on, a haunted meat loaf?"

Mike Burger grabbed a string bean from someone's plate and dangled it in front of Roy.

"I'm coming to get you, Roy!" Mike cried. "I will come after you in your sleep!"

"Oh, no!" Roy threw his arms up in the air. "Please don't hurt me, Mr. String Bean! Pleeeze!"

Mike grabbed the picture out of the Polaroid and held it up for everyone to see.

There I was, my eyes popping with fear, gravy stains all over my shirt.

I've never looked so stupid in my life.

"Give me that!" I snapped. I tried ripping the photo out of Mike's hands, but he was too tall.

The Burger brothers walked away, laughing. Penny smirked at me. "When are you ever going to learn that there's no such thing as ghosts?" she asked.

I stepped up and stared her in the eye. "Wait until tomorrow, Penny. I'll get you back!"

"Oooh, I'm so scared. Your lame attempt at revenge will have to wait. I won't be here tomorrow. I think I'm coming down with something." Tossing her red curls, Penny sauntered away.

I slumped down into my seat and put my head in my hands. "Oh, man, this is the worst day I've ever had!" I groaned. "I can't look. Is everyone still staring at me?"

"Well . . . not *everyone*," Connor told me.

I sighed. "I wish I were invisible."

"Jack!" Connor gasped.

I lifted my head. "What?"

Connor stared off past my shoulder. The expression on his face gave me chills.

"Jack! Jack!" he called. "Where did you go?"

"What do you mean? I'm right here!"

"Where?"

"Here!" I waved my hands in front of Connor's face.

But he didn't seem to see them.

"Your wish," he whispered. "It came true."

"Huh?"

"Jack," Connor said solemnly. "You're invisible."

2

Invisible? Me?

My mouth went dry all of a sudden. Could it be?

I stuck my hands in front of my face.

I could still see them.

I glanced down at my feet. Still there.

"I can see myself," I whispered. "Are you sure you can't see me, Connor? Not even a little bit?"

Connor's shoulders hunched in a jerky motion. A weird snorting noise came out of his nose.

I stared at him. Was he having some kind of fit?

Then he burst out laughing.

"Oh," he gasped. "Oh, man. I really had you going!"

"You are *sooo* funny," I growled. "Really. I mean that."

"Sorry," he apologized. "I just couldn't resist. Oh, man, the look on your face!"

I scowled and stood up. "Thanks a lot, *buddy.*"

"Oh, come on. You know I'm just kidding."

I bussed my tray. I'd have to go hungry. I just didn't feel like looking at that meat loaf anymore.

Things got worse after lunch.

As Connor and I walked down the hall to class, I noticed some papers taped to the lockers.

I strolled closer to peer at one of them.

My heart sank. This couldn't be happening.

The Burger brothers must have snuck into the art room. They had made dozens of copies of that dumb picture of me in the cafeteria.

The copies were blown up in all sizes. And they were all over. On the door of the boys' room. On the lockers. On the water fountain. Everywhere I looked I saw my stupid expression.

I'm doomed! I realized. The whole school is going to think I'm a first-class loser.

"Boy, those guys just don't quit," Connor remarked, ripping one of the copies from a locker door.

"I can't believe what a nightmare this is. We've got to get them all off!" I cried.

I raced from locker to locker, tearing them down.

Connor pulled the photo off the boys' room door. "I'll see if there are any more in here."

He emerged with a crumpled handful. We tossed them into the garbage.

"Maybe no one looked at them," Connor suggested.

"Are you kidding? They were everywhere!" I moaned.

Then it hit me. The girls' room! They must be all over the girls' room.

I ran to the girls' room door. Then I stopped. Wait a second. I couldn't go in there!

The door opened. Karen Harris and Brittany Carson came out. They took one look at me and burst out laughing.

Strike two with Brittany.

As they walked down the hall, I banged my head against one of the lockers.

"Come on," Connor urged. "Penny and the Burger brothers are not worth it, Jack. Let's get to class."

I lowered my head and shuffled down the hall, taking down the pictures wherever I saw them.

Kids came up to me as I walked into class and patted me on the back.

"Nice picture, Jacko," Kirk Russ said.

"Yeah, I'm going to have one framed!" Andrew Griffin shouted.

I peered around the classroom. Brittany glanced up as I walked in. Then she lowered her eyes again quickly.

I couldn't blame her for thinking I was a loser.

I slid into my usual desk and cracked open my textbook, pretending to read it. But all I could think about was how I wished this day would end.

I felt for my lucky spider ring, then realized again that I had left it at home.

11

"Okay, everyone, settle down," Ms. Beamus called. She's one of those no-nonsense teachers who never cracks a smile.

She tapped on her desk with her ruler until everyone quieted down. Then she wrote a problem on the board. "Who wants to work this one out?"

Connor's hand shot up. Ms. Beamus ignored him because he always has the right answers.

I stared at my textbook, hoping she wouldn't call on me.

"How about you, Jack?" she asked.

"Huh?" I mumbled. Brilliant.

"Why don't you work out this problem on the board?" Ms. Beamus asked firmly.

Couldn't she see that I'd had enough humiliation for one day? Plus I still had gravy on my shirt from my accident with Mr. Lincoln.

I stood up slowly. The room was quiet.

"It's easy," Connor whispered.

Of course Connor thought it was easy.

Ms. Beamus walked to the back of the room. I stared at the problem on the board.

And stared. And stared.

I had no idea how to solve it.

I couldn't just walk back to my seat. So I picked up the chalk and tried scribbling some numbers on the board. My fingers were sweating so much, the chalk slipped out of my hand.

I bent down to pick up the chalk and heard

12

someone whisper, "I am the ghost of the chalk!" A few kids snickered.

I could swear that Brittany was one of them.

"That's not the correct answer, Jack," Ms. Beamus said. "Why don't you try again?"

Again! Was she kidding me? What made her think I'd be able to do it now?

For what seemed like the millionth time, I wished I were invisible.

Just like that. Poof! Nonexistent.

Beads of sweat covered my forehead. I wiped them away with my sleeve and tried again.

Still no luck. I faced Ms. Beamus and shrugged. "I can't do it," I confessed.

Ms. Beamus sniffed. "Maybe if you paid more attention in class, you'd know how to figure it out, Jack."

I stood there, staring down at the floor. No question. This was definitely the worst day of my entire life.

I had to get Penny back. And Mike and Roy.

I needed to show the seventh grade I wasn't a total geek.

I kept going over the day in my head as I walked back home with Connor. He tried to make me feel better. "I know you had a bummer day. But forget about it."

"Oh, yeah!" I snapped. "Easy for you to say. *You*

didn't spill your lunch on Mr. Lincoln. *You* didn't have a conversation with your lunch. And you know how to solve any math problem."

Connor looked offended. "First, I watch where I'm walking. Second, Penny and those guys know better than to pull that kind of joke on me—"

"Sure," I interrupted. "Like you would have figured it out."

"I would have looked for a logical explanation," he retorted. "You have to stop being so jumpy about supernatural stuff. People know they can get you."

"You and your logic," I grumbled.

Still, I knew Connor was right. I had to shake this reputation for being some kind of scaredy-cat.

I had to be more like Connor. Instead of getting scared, I had to *think*.

"Okay." I faced him. "I'm turning over a new leaf. The new Jack Meyers doesn't believe in ghosts!"

Connor clapped me on my back. "Excellent! Now, let's cut through the Fear Street Cemetery. It's faster."

I stopped short and gaped at him. "Are you nuts?" I asked. "No one in their right mind cuts through there."

Connor was trying to balance his backpack on his head. He stopped. The backpack slipped off. He caught it in midair and gazed at me.

"I thought you didn't believe in ghosts anymore. Aren't you the new Jack Meyers?"

I swallowed hard.

All those stories about Fear Street and everything were probably just that—stories. Probably kids like Penny made them up to scare people. Right?

The cemetery was only a few feet away. It gave me chills just to look at it. Swirls of thick gray mist curled around the tombstones. It looked like something out of an old horror movie.

I hesitated. "I don't know. . . ."

"Don't be a wimp," Connor warned.

There's nothing I hate more than being called a wimp.

"Fine," I said. "Let's do it."

I stared at the silent cemetery. It was growing foggier.

Something howled in the distance.

My stomach tightened. A weird chill crawled up my arms and legs.

Maybe this wasn't such a good idea.

"Come on." Connor pulled open the iron gate. "I'm going to prove to you that there are no such things as ghosts."

I squared my shoulders. "Okay," I said, trying to keep my voice from shaking. "Let's go."

3

Everything was quiet. Really quiet.

Fog flowed around me so thick, I could barely see my hand in front of my face.

"In this fog I really do feel invisible," I murmured.

My feet sank into the ground as I walked. It felt as if I were being pulled down into the earth. As if something were yanking me into its grave.

Something dead.

I started breathing hard. Sweat trickled down my sides.

Why did I let Connor bring me here?

I bumped into something hard.

"Ouch!" I cried. I peered down, rubbing my shin.

I had bumped into a small tombstone. It was so old, the letters were worn away. But I could read the date—1823.

Black, gnarled trees poked up out of the ground like wicked fingers. Wilted flowers surrounded some tombstones.

Connor stopped in the middle of the cemetery and glanced around. "See? No ghosts," he said. "Just a plain old cemetery."

"Okay, I get your point." I pulled on his jacket. "Now, let's go. I'm late."

And totally scared. But I didn't want Connor to know that.

"Look at that old tomb!" Connor cried, pointing a few feet ahead of us. "It's a whole house."

"It's called a mausoleum," I told him. "My grandfather was buried in something like that."

The mausoleum loomed above the fog. It was a huge gray structure, bigger than my room at home. Cracked stone steps led up to a heavy stone door.

I didn't like the looks of it. At all.

"What do you think is in there?" Connor asked.

I shrugged. "Dead bodies, I guess."

"Cool," Connor murmured.

Just then, out of the corner of my eye, I saw something move. I whipped my head around. My eyes frantically searched the cemetery.

No one there.

At least, not that I could see. But I had a funny feeling. A feeling that eyes were watching me. Staring at me.

Boring a hole right through me.

"What's with you?" Connor asked.

17

"Nothing, I just—"

Something rustled behind me. Was someone creeping up on us?

"Who's there?" I demanded.

Connor stared at me as if I were nuts. "I didn't hear anything," he said.

I heard the rustling sound again. It sounded like someone walking on dead leaves.

I glanced nervously around.

Where was it? Where was it?

"Jack! Look out!" Connor screamed.

I spun around just in time to see a huge dark creature barreling toward me.

4

The creature knocked me to the ground. I felt its hot breath blast in my face.

I squeezed my eyes shut. "Get off!" I screamed, shoving the creature to one side.

I heard it scramble on the leaves, then whimper.

I opened my eyes.

Hey! It was a dog. A huge black, drooling, scared-to-death dog. It let out another, louder whimper.

Then it darted away into the fog.

Connor rushed over to me.

"Are you okay?" he asked.

"Yeah, just startled." I stared after the dog, rubbing my chest where he slammed into me.

"Something really freaked him out," Connor remarked. "I wonder what it was?"

"Let's get out of here," I whispered. "This place gives me the creeps."

I adjusted my backpack on my shoulders and started walking toward the other end of the cemetery.

"Hang on," Connor called. "I want to check out that mausoleum for a second."

My heart seemed to rise in my chest. Why did Connor have to push our luck?

Something was out there.

Watching.

Waiting.

Scaring dogs.

I just wanted to get out of there and go home. But Connor wanted to check out a creepy building full of dead bodies!

"Just for a second," Connor repeated. "Promise."

I watched as he climbed the steps to the mausoleum. He stopped and stared at something near the door.

My heart thudded in my chest as I waited for him. "Let's *go,*" I muttered, stomping my feet to warm them up.

It wasn't this cold earlier today. I didn't even zip up my jacket when we were walking home from school.

But for some reason the cemetery was freezing.

Connor didn't budge. "Come here." He motioned me over. "Look at this."

"What is it?" I demanded.

"Just come here," he insisted. "You've got to see this."

Connor could be really stubborn. I knew the only way I was going to get out of there was to check out that dumb mausoleum. That, or leave Connor and go through the cemetery alone.

I wasn't about to do that.

I took a deep breath and climbed the steps.

Connor pointed to a carving on the stone door. A face. A girl's face. Beneath the face was a weird poem:

> *For years and years*
> *I've lived in stone*
> *But you can set me free.*
> *Kiss my lips*
> *To bring me back*
> *That is my only plea.*

The wind howled, sending shivers across my skin.

I couldn't move. I just kept staring at that pretty, sad-eyed face. How could a stone carving seem so real?

"So why don't you kiss it?" Connor teased.

"Huh?" I almost forgot he was there.

"Kiss the face," Connor said. "Come on, do it."

"That's the dumbest thing you have ever asked me to do," I grumbled.

"What's the matter?" Connor poked me. "Afraid it's going to come true?"

I read the words again. What if it were true? What if kissing it brought some horrible creature to life?

Plus, what if someone was watching?

How stupid would I look kissing a slab of stone?

I shot Connor a suspicious look. "Hold on a minute. Are the Burger brothers waiting somewhere to take my picture if I kiss the stone?" I asked.

"Give me a break!" Connor exclaimed. "I'm your best friend!"

He had a point. He might tease me. But he would never set me up to embarrass me.

I laughed. The whole thing was dumb. Plus, Connor was being stubborn again. There was only one way I'd get him to leave.

I'd have to kiss the stone face.

"Come on," Connor urged. "You're the new Jack Meyers, remember? Just do it. That way I'll know you aren't afraid."

"Okay, okay." I rolled my eyes. "Here goes."

I leaned in close. Then I stopped.

This was so stupid!

I turned to Connor. He gazed back at me expectantly.

I couldn't believe he wanted me to kiss a piece of stone. But I had to be the new Jack Meyers. The one who wasn't afraid of anything.

Plus, this wasn't really scary. It was just embarrassing.

And I was used to being embarrassed.
I squeezed my eyes shut and held my breath.
My lips touched the stone lips of the carving.
My eyes flew open.
I jumped backward.
"Her lips!" I gasped. "They—they're warm!"

5

"**C**onnor!" I cried, grabbing his arm. "Her lips are warm!"

I shuddered. I could still feel it—the touch of warm flesh when I expected only cold stone.

"What?" Connor stared at me.

"Warm! Warm!" My voice squeaked. "She's alive, man! Let's get out of here!"

"Come on, Jack." Connor rolled his eyes. "She's not alive. She's not even a *she*. She's an *it*—a stone carving. Look at it!"

I forced myself to stare at the carved face.

I had to admit, it looked like stone.

"Touch it," I whispered to Connor.

He reached out and poked the carving in the cheek.

"Cold," he informed me. "Cold and hard." He shook his head. "The new Jack Meyers. Hah!"

I felt a flush creeping up my neck.

I had done it again. Made a geek of myself.

"Okay, let's go," Connor said finally.

We went down the steps and started to walk away.

I heard something creak behind me. I stopped.

It sounded like a door.

"Come on, Jack," Connor said impatiently.

Obviously, he didn't hear anything. I began walking again.

The only door around here was the mausoleum door.

But there was no one in there to open it.

No one alive, anyway.

I picked up my pace.

"Wait! Stop, please!" called a voice.

This time we both heard it. A girl's voice.

Connor and I stopped and turned around slowly.

In front of the mausoleum stood a girl.

My mouth dropped open as I stared at her. She beckoned to us with a long, pale hand.

She seemed about our age, maybe a little older.

And she looked an awful lot like the stone face I kissed.

My mouth moved—but no words came out.

"It's her!" I finally whispered.

She glided toward us. The wind whipped her blond hair around her face.

Her eyes locked onto mine. They were the same color as her velvet dress—a deep dark blue. She didn't

25

speak. She just kept staring at me with those sad blue eyes.

Who was she? Where did she come from?

Was she a ghost?

I took a step back. I wanted to run.

I wanted to run fast and never look back.

But my feet were frozen to the spot.

"What do you want?" Connor demanded.

She smiled. "My name is Luana. I come from a different time," she told us calmly. "And a different place."

She stared at me again. Tiny shivers ran up my spine.

But I couldn't say a word.

"Hundreds of years ago my family and I were servants of a powerful sorcerer. Powerful and evil," the girl continued. She paused and gazed off into space.

Connor nudged me with his elbow. "Yeah, sure. And I'm actually from the planet Pluto," he whispered to me.

Luana snapped back to attention. "Please don't joke with me. I'm quite serious," she said sternly.

"Oh, sorry." Connor got a patient look on his face, the one he got when he thought I was being dumb. "Tell us more."

Luana went on. "This evil sorcerer caught me in his precious library, reading his spell books. He was furious. The secrets of his magic were not for a servant like me."

She paused for breath. I glanced uncertainly at Connor.

He still had that patient look on his face.

He wasn't buying any of it.

"The sorcerer imprisoned me in this tomb," she continued, pointing to the mausoleum. "I was to live out my days here—until someone freed me with a kiss."

She held her hand out to me. "Thank you. You saved me from an eternity in stone."

I didn't want to touch her. I didn't want to have anything to do with her. It was all too spooky.

But she kept holding out her hand to me. At last I grabbed it and gave it a quick squeeze.

It was warm. She was definitely real—not a ghost. I breathed a sigh of relief.

"Now I need your help once again," she said. "Please help me get back to my time and my family. Please."

Connor nudged me with his elbow. "Come on, Jack. Let's get out of here." He glared at Luana. "I bet the Burger brothers put you up to this stupid trick. Or maybe Penny."

"It is not a trick!" Luana cried. "And I don't know anyone named Penny. Or the Burger brothers. Please believe me."

"Let's go, Jack," Connor urged. He tugged on my arm.

I pulled away from him. "I don't know." I glanced

27

at the face on the door. "That's her face carved there."

Connor grabbed my arm again. "It *isn't* her. It could be any girl. Let's go."

Luana stared at me with her sad eyes. I felt as though she could see right through me.

"This is dumb. I'm out of here," Connor grumbled. He started to walk away.

I hurried after him. "What if she's telling the truth?" I asked in a low voice. "She came out of the mausoleum."

Connor didn't stop walking. "Jack, you are hopeless. Did you see the tomb door open?"

"No," I admitted lamely. "But I heard a noise—"

"But you didn't *see* it," Connor broke in. "I'm telling you, she followed us here. She was just waiting for a chance to play a trick on you. Don't fall for it!"

I sighed. Connor's explanation did make sense.

"I guess," I agreed at last.

We kept walking. We were almost at the cemetery gate when I heard running footsteps behind us.

"Wait!" Luana called. "If you help me, maybe there is something I can do for you in return."

I spun to face her. Enough of this weird girl!

"Like what?" I sneered.

Connor folded his arms. "Yeah. Like what?"

"I have powers," Luana said breathlessly. "I learned many things when I sneaked into the sorcerer's library. Things that you might be interested in."

"Look," I started to say. "This all sounds very interesting, but—"

She kept talking. "I can change rocks into water. I can make it rain. I can turn things invisible. I can make a dog fly—"

"Yeah, sure!" I laughed. Even *I* could tell now that Luana was lying. No way could she do all that stuff! "Hey, I know. I've been wishing I were invisible all day. If you're so powerful, make me invisible!"

Luana shrugged. "Fine. I'll do it!"

6

"I'll make you invisible. It's easy," Luana told us.

She sounded so sure of herself! For a second I felt shaken. Could she really do it?

No way! The new Jack knew better, I reminded myself. The new Jack could take a joke. But he wouldn't be fooled.

"Okay, Luana," I challenged. "We're ready. Make us both invisible. Me and Connor."

"All right," Luana said calmly.

She raised her face up to the sky and closed her eyes. I could see her lips moving quickly. But no words came out.

Her face was so serious. Again I felt that little thrill of doubt.

Was it possible?

Could she really make us invisible?

Connor leaned over. "She's some kind of nut," he whispered in my ear. "I think she really believes she's magic! Let's get out of here." He pulled the rusty iron cemetery gate open.

Luana's eyes snapped open. "By morning you will be invisible. But only from sunup to sundown. Remember that."

Connor was already through the gate.

"Whatever you say," I told Luana quickly. "Uh—thanks!"

I sprinted to catch up to Connor.

"She was too weird," I said when I caught up with him.

"Yeah," Connor agreed. "Talk about a freak show."

But in the back of my mind, I couldn't help wondering.

Maybe, just maybe . . .

At dinner, I sat thinking about my day. The embarrassment at school. The weird girl in the cemetery.

"Hey, Space Case," my elder sister, Carrie, snapped. She threw her napkin at me. "Look alive."

"Carrie, can't you leave your brother alone?" my mom asked wearily.

"Mom, he's like a zombie or something. Look at him," Carrie complained.

"Bug off, will you?" I grumbled. "I just don't feel like talking nonstop about totally stupid things."

Carrie glared at me.

The phone rang as I was clearing the table.

Carrie answered. When I came out of the kitchen, she tossed the cordless at me. "It's your loser friend, Connor."

"So—invisible yet?" he teased when I picked the phone up.

"Yeah, right. Remember—it's not supposed to happen until sunup," I joked back. "But I'm ready, man."

We talked for a few minutes, but then I hung up because Carrie kept bugging me to get off the phone.

After I cleaned up, I watched my favorite show on TV and did my homework. Then I went to bed.

As I lay there in the dark, I sighed. Even though I was the new Jack Meyers now, I still wished I could really be invisible tomorrow. After the day I had, I didn't know how I could ever show my face at school again.

I picked up my spider ring, which was sitting on my night table. "You'd better bring me better luck tomorrow," I whispered.

I slipped the ring on so I wouldn't forget to wear it in the morning.

Maybe I didn't believe in ghosts anymore. But I still believed in taking precautions for good luck!

The alarm clock startled me the next morning. I rubbed the sleep out of my eyes and unwrapped myself from my sheets.

The floor felt cold on my bare feet. I shoved my feet into my slippers and stumbled down the hall.

As I approached the bathroom, I heard Carrie's alarm go off. I locked the bathroom door so she couldn't barge in.

Then I peered blearily into the mirror.

Huh? Something was wrong.

I rubbed my eyes again. And again.

Hey! Where was I?

I had no reflection!

None!

I stared down at myself.

Nothing there. No feet. No arms. Nothing.

I brought my hand up to my face.

It couldn't be.

But it was.

I was invisible!

7

I couldn't believe it. I was completely invisible!

Luana really did it!

I peered down at myself again. I wiggled my right foot around. Couldn't see it.

I made a face at myself in the mirror. Nothing.

No matter what I did, I stayed invisible.

This was *too* cool.

Then it hit me.

Connor must be invisible too! I had to go and find him.

"Jack, get out of there—now!" Carrie shouted. She pounded on the bathroom door like she did every morning.

"Come on, Jack! What is taking you so long? You are worse than a girl!"

I felt a smile spread across my face. I had a great idea. An idea that would make Carrie wish she never said that.

I washed my invisible face and brushed my invisible teeth. I was careful to make lots of noise. I even gargled.

This was going to be a great day.

A great *invisible* day.

Carrie was still yelling. "You'd better be out of there by the time I count to three! One, two, th—"

I opened the door calmly.

Carrie peered into the bathroom. Then her face bunched up in anger.

"Where are you, you little creep?" she demanded. "I know you're in here!"

I stepped aside as she stalked over to the tub. She yanked the shower curtain aside.

"Very funny, Jack. I know you're in here. I heard you brushing your teeth. Now, come out so I can give you a pounding."

Like *that* would make me come out of hiding.

Carrie got down on her knees and peeked under the sink. She stood up, shaking her head.

"That little brat," she muttered.

I quietly sneaked out of the bathroom and crept into Carrie's room while she brushed her teeth. When I spotted her fancy antique doll, I got another great idea.

I never understood why she kept that dumb old doll

35

anyway. She never played with it, not even when she was little. She just kept it on a shelf in its frilly little costume. Mom says it's a collector's item.

I thought it would make a great action figure.

Carrie walked into her room brushing her hair. Her hair is nothing special. It's just brown and kind of long. But she brushes it a million times a day anyway.

"Quit brushing your hair!" I said in a high, squeaky voice. "You're going to make it fall out!"

Carrie threw her brush down on her dresser and spun around.

"This idiotic game of yours is getting pretty boring, Jack," she sneered. She stomped over to her bed and pulled up the dust ruffle.

"Over here, stupid," I said in the same squeaky voice.

Carrie stood up slowly and searched her room in confusion.

I grabbed the doll's arm and made it wave up and down.

"Hi, dummy!" I squeaked.

The color drained out of Carrie's face.

"Jack?" she asked hesitantly.

"Do I look like a Jack to you, dimwit?" I squeaked.

Carrie backed away, staring at her doll.

I made it jump off the shelf and start walking toward her.

"I'm sick of this outfit," I whined. "Why can't you

36

dress me in something decent? I hate this ugly dress! I hate it!"

Carrie backed into her dresser. She shook her head in disbelief.

"And another thing—" I began to say.

"*Mom!*" Carrie screamed. She jumped up onto her bed. "Come quick!"

I dropped the doll as soon as I heard my mom's footsteps pounding down the hall. She dashed in.

"What on earth is the matter?" she demanded. "Carrie, why are you standing on your bed?"

"M-m-my doll! It was talking to me! And it w-walked toward me!" Carrie stammered.

I clapped my hand over my mouth to keep from cracking up.

My mother sighed. "Nice try. But you can drop the hysterical act. You're going to school today, Carrie. Now, you'd better get ready to go."

Carrie didn't budge. She just kept staring at her doll.

"It really happened!" she wailed. "She told me she didn't like her outfit! She said it was ugly! It's true, Mom!"

I knew if I didn't get out of her room soon, I was going to lose it. I sneaked out quietly.

I had to find Connor. But I felt funny in my pajamas, even if I was invisible.

I crept down the hall and slipped into my room. I

pulled some clothes out of my closet and tossed them on the bed. Then I took off my pajamas.

As soon as the pajamas were off my body, they started appearing again.

Whoa. Way cool.

I put on a sock. Once it was on my foot, it faded away until it totally disappeared.

I took it off again. Presto—it appeared!

Unbelievable!

I did the same thing with my shirt. It was so cool to watch. But I knew I had to get out of there fast. So I finished dressing and headed down the hall. I could hear my mom arguing with Carrie as I bounded down the stairs.

"Bye, Mom," I called out from the bottom of the stairs. "Gotta get to school early today!"

"Okay," she called back.

This was so excellent!

Now I had to pick Connor up. I knew I'd have ten times more fun if Connor and I were both invisible.

The day was crisp and cold. I raced around the corner to Connor's house. His dog, Mutt, barked when I rang the doorbell.

"Coming!" Connor's mom called from inside the house.

She opened the door and peered out.

"Hello?" she asked.

Mutt stood by her side, barking his head off.

"Hi, Mrs. Craig," I greeted her. "Is Connor home?"

But I forgot one thing.

Mrs. Craig couldn't see me.

Her eyes grew wide. She stared around the porch.

"Who's there?" she demanded. "Where are you?"

I gulped and stepped backward. The porch creaked.

"Who's there? Answer me!" Mrs. Craig commanded. "Answer me right now!"

8

"**W**hoever you are, this is not funny," Mrs. Craig snapped. "Come out where I can see you."

She walked out onto her porch. Mutt raced over to me and planted his front paws on my chest.

"Mutt, what is the matter with you?" Mrs. Craig asked, staring at the big dog. "What are you doing?"

Oh, man! Mutt must look pretty strange standing on his hind legs like that. I tried to push him away. But he wouldn't budge.

Mrs. Craig gazed at Mutt in amazement. "I've never seen you do this before," she murmured. "It's some trick."

Then Mutt started licking my face with his big, sloppy tongue. I hate it when he does that.

"Yuck!" I muttered, wiping my face with my sleeve.

Mrs. Craig put her hands on her hips. "All right. I

heard that. Where are you?" she demanded, glaring around in a circle.

I knew I had to get out of there, and fast.

While Connor's mom was hunting around the porch, I got Mutt off me and crept into the house. I could still hear Mrs. Craig talking to no one as I sprinted up the stairs.

"Connor?" I called quietly. "Connor, are you invisible?"

How do you find an invisible person anyway? I wondered.

I pushed Connor's bedroom door open a crack and peered inside. No one was there. At least not that I could see.

"Where are you?" I whispered. "Connor, are you in here?"

All was quiet. Maybe Connor didn't turn invisible. Maybe he was already at school.

That would be a real bummer.

I turned to leave. And bumped my head right into something hard. Like a chin.

"Ouch!" I cried, rubbing my forehead.

"Watch where you're going!" a familiar voice said.

"Connor! It's you!"

"Who else would it be?" Connor said.

I reached out toward his voice. I could feel something with my finger, but I had no idea what it was.

"Hey, get your finger out of my nose," Connor complained.

Ugh. "Sorry," I said.

41

"I can't believe it actually worked," Connor said. "This is too cool. I've been doing funny stuff to my parents all morning. They can't figure out what's going on."

I laughed, thinking of Carrie with her dumb doll.

"Can you give me a logical explanation for this one?" I asked. "Come on, tell the truth."

"No." Connor sighed. "But I'm working on it."

"So I'm not so dumb for believing in the supernatural, then," I pressed.

"I guess not," Connor admitted. "So—what should we do now? I mean, there's no point in going to school. Even if we go, they won't be able to see us. We'll be marked absent."

"Hey, you're right." I never thought of that.

An invisible grin spread across my face as I considered the possibilities. We could do *anything!* Sneak into the movieplex and watch movies for free! Sneak into the girls' locker room!

Then I had it. A great idea. And a way to pay Penny Morris back for the trick she played on me yesterday.

"Come with me," I told Connor. "I know exactly what to do."

9

We left Connor's house by the back door. Believe it or not, his mom was *still* out on the front porch, searching for me. I held in a laugh as we walked past her.

We walked down Melinda Lane, then turned onto MacDonald Way. Penny's puke-pink house came into sight.

"Penny said she was going to fake being sick today," I reminded Connor. "I think we should pay her a little visit. A little *ghostly* visit."

"Awesome!" Connor cried.

We stopped and stood on the sidewalk. I stared at her window, thinking of all the ways I could freak her out.

This was going to be great.

"Let's go inside," I told Connor. "When I clear my throat, that's the signal to get out."

"Got it."

Luckily, the front door was unlocked. I could hear Penny's mom on the phone in the kitchen. We crept up to Penny's room.

She lay in bed. Cold medicine and a glass of orange juice sat on her nightstand. She was watching cartoons on a small TV.

I tiptoed to the TV and changed the channel to some dumb talk show.

"Huh?" Penny said. She picked up the remote and stared at it. Then she turned back to the cartoons.

I stifled a laugh and turned back to the talk show.

Penny jiggled the remote. "Mom!" she called. "Something's wrong with the TV."

I started changing stations like crazy. Penny kept jabbing the remote with her finger, trying to turn back to the cartoons.

"What is up with this stupid TV?" she mumbled. Finally she sighed and turned it off.

I turned it back on and cranked up the volume. Really loud.

Penny sat straight up in bed, staring around.

Then Connor turned on Penny's radio. Full blast.

Penny's eyes were huge, like two softballs in her head. She pulled her covers up around her chin.

I crept to Penny's desk and turned on her computer. I typed HELLO, PENNY. ARE YOU REALLY SICK? OR

44

DID YOU JUST WANT TO GET OUT OF THE MATH QUIZ TODAY?

Penny gasped. "Who's in here?" she demanded.

I deleted the other message and typed in DO YOU BELIEVE IN GHOSTS, PENNY? :-(

"M-Mom!" Penny shouted.

I quickly tore a page out of her notebook and folded it into a paper airplane. I zoomed it straight into her forehead.

"Mom! Help!" Penny yelled.

Connor started opening and closing her bureau drawers while I bombed her with more paper airplanes.

Penny stood up on her bed with her covers wrapped tightly around her. Her face was as white as her sheets.

If only I had a picture of *that!*

Then I heard Penny's mom climbing the stairs. Time to go.

I cleared my throat loudly. I felt Connor's jacket brush against my arm as he crept by me. I slid past Penny's mom and raced down the stairs.

I saw the door open in front of me. Connor was out.

"Connor?" I whispered as soon as I stepped outside.

I heard him laughing. He was already on the sidewalk.

"That computer message was genius!" he cried.

I had to admit it was a pretty cool trick. Penny was

definitely going to think twice the next time she decided to tease me about ghosts!

"Let's go to school," Connor suggested as we strolled down the street.

"I thought you said there was no point in us going," I objected.

"I changed my mind. First of all, we could sneak into the office and take our names off the absentee list." Connor laughed. "Second, I have a feeling we could have a lot of fun being invisible in school."

I grinned. "All right!"

So we went to school. Our first stop was the principal's office. Teachers send the absentee lists there after first period. Then the school secretary writes a note to the parents. Checking up on us.

We waited until Ms. Shavers, the secretary, stepped out for a second. Then we went in and erased our names from the list. I checked Ms. Shavers's desk. She hadn't written the notes yet.

"I know," Connor whispered, chuckling. I watched his pencil reverse itself in midair. It seemed to write on the absentee list by magic.

I peered down at the list. In place of our names, Connor had written "Mike Burger" and "Roy Burger."

Perfect revenge. The Burger brothers would be in big trouble when they got home from school.

We crept out of the office and into the empty hallway.

"Good thinking!" I told Connor as we walked down the hall. "Where to now?"

"I need to make a pit stop," Connor told me.

The bell rang. We quickly ducked into the boys' room.

A moment later the door opened again. Two boys came in, talking and laughing.

I recognized the voices immediately.

The Burger brothers!

"I guess Meyers doesn't dare show his face around here after what we did to him," Roy was saying.

Mike laughed. "Yeah," he agreed. "What a wimp."

They were talking about me!

I'd show them.

I started to flush the toilet in my stall over and over. Then I slipped into another stall and flushed that one too.

Connor must have picked up on what I was doing, because then I heard flushes coming from three more stalls.

"What's going on?" Roy asked.

"I don't know." Mike sounded worried. "It sounds like the toilets are going to explode."

I raced over to the sink and turned on all the faucets. I splashed water in Roy's and Mike's faces.

Connor balled up paper towels and lobbed them at the Burger brothers.

"Wh-what's h-h-happening!" Roy stuttered.

Then I picked up a roll of toilet paper and watched

47

with delight as Roy's and Mike's eyes grew wider and wider.

They gasped as the floating toilet paper unwound. I started to wrap it around Roy's head. Connor took another roll and wrapped it around Mike's feet as he stood there, frozen.

"Hey! Cut it out! Leave me alone!" Roy yelled.

"Let's get out of here!" Mike screamed.

They scrambled to the door.

I decided to be a gentleman and open it for them. But then I tripped them on their way out.

The only sight I've seen more ridiculous than my blown-up fright face was right there in front of me.

Mike and Roy Burger lay sprawled on the floor in the hall, covered in toilet paper.

People in the hallway stopped, pointed, and howled with laughter.

I loved every second of it.

Maybe yesterday was the worst day of my life.

But today was turning out to be the *best* day of my life!

10

Being invisible at school was more fun than anything I could imagine. We goofed around all morning. Before we knew it, the lunch bell rang.

"Hungry?" I asked Connor.

"Of course," he replied.

"Well, I don't want any of the cafeteria food," I said. "Hey, I know! We could order a pizza and have them deliver it to the teachers' lounge."

"Won't work," Connor objected. "How could we pay for it?"

"Oh, yeah. What a drag," I grumbled.

"But let's check out the teachers' lounge anyway," Connor suggested. "Maybe they keep snacks in there. It's worth a try."

We followed Ms. Beamus in. I had never been to the

teachers' lounge before, and I didn't know what to expect.

I always thought that it would be clean and cozy, with carpeting, a VCR, stuff like that.

Boy, was I mistaken.

The teachers' lounge looked like a classroom, with old, stained, mismatched furniture instead of desks and chairs. No VCR. No stereo. Just a microwave oven that looked as if they picked it up at a yard sale.

The room smelled like burnt coffee and stale cigarettes. Newspapers and magazines were piled up everywhere.

It was a total mess!

Mr. Kopnick sat down in a ratty old armchair and picked up the paper. He dug through it until he found the comics. He giggled as he read the first page.

Ms. Parma sat at a table grading papers. She did not look happy. I peered over her shoulder to see whose paper she was grading.

It was Penny's. She was getting a C−.

Hah! Penny was always bragging about her grades.

Beside me, Connor's stomach growled loudly.

Uh-oh! Time to search for some food.

Ms. Beamus was eating a salad she must have brought from home. Boring!

Mr. Kopnick was picking at some fruit. Another lame lunch.

I peered over his head at Ms. Parma.

Hmm. *She* had a plateful of French-bread pizza. It

was steaming gently. She must have brought it from home and microwaved it.

Now, *that* looked good!

I perched on the chair next to hers. Maybe I could sneak a piece when she wasn't looking.

The door opened and Mr. Lincoln stepped into the room. He was carrying a tray with today's cafeteria offering: a sad-looking, soggy lasagna.

I guess he decided to eat here today, away from flying meat loaf.

I turned my attention back to Ms. Parma's pizza. Maybe if I could get Connor to create a distraction . . .

Then a shadow fell across me. I glanced up.

Oh, no! Mr. Lincoln stood by my chair.

He obviously thought it was empty.

But it wasn't. *I* was in it.

And he was going to sit right on me!

I quickly shoved the chair back and stood up.

Mr. Lincoln was already in sitting position. He let out a yelp and fell to the floor. Right on his rear end.

I clapped my hand over my mouth. He had dumped his tray all over himself.

Mr. Lincoln was wearing his lunch for the second day in a row!

I heard Connor laugh. I couldn't help it. I started cracking up too.

"Are you all right?" Ms. Parma cried. She helped Mr. Lincoln to his feet.

The other teachers stared around frantically. I could see the confusion on their faces. They were baffled. Where did the laughter come from?

"Who's there?" Mr. Kopnick called.

Then I felt an itch in my nose.

Oh, no. Not now, please.

My nose itched again. I scratched it, but it didn't make any difference.

I had to get out of there, fast.

Before I totally blew our cover.

I was going to sneeze!

In all the commotion, it was actually easy to get out of the teachers' lounge. I sneezed just as I made it out to the hallway.

"Bless you," I heard Connor whisper.

Then I noticed two pieces of French-bread pizza hovering in midair.

Yes! Connor snagged us some lunch!

"Give me one of those," I whispered. "I'm starving!"

We strolled down the empty hall, munching our pizza. I watched as bites disappeared out of Connor's slice. It looked like one of those cool special effects.

Connor began to laugh.

"I can't believe you nailed Mr. Lincoln again!"

I started to laugh again too.

"That's what he gets for eating the cafeteria food!" We were having too much fun!

The day kept getting better. We started a food fight in the cafeteria. And we made things float during band practice. Everyone in the band thought the auditorium was really haunted.

Finally we decided we wanted to be invisible somewhere besides school. So we left.

I glanced up at the sky as we walked. The sun was low in the west. We didn't have much time left before we turned visible again. And I wanted our last adventure to be great.

Then I spotted a familiar brick building in front of us.

The community pool! It was closed on Thursdays. But I bet it would be easy for a couple of invisible guys to sneak in. . . .

"Hey, Connor, want to go for a swim?" I asked.

"Great idea!" he said.

We cruised around the building, looking for an entrance.

"Jack!" Connor exclaimed. "Look. The back door is open!"

Sure enough, it was ajar. A white van was parked nearby. Somebody must be making a delivery or something.

Connor and I stepped inside and walked cautiously down the hall to the pool.

It was eerily quiet. I was so used to having a ton of

other kids splashing around in it. But now the water lay still and silent. The big overhead lights were shut off.

We had the entire pool all to ourselves.

I heard a screech and a splash. Connor was already in.

"Come on, Jack!" he called. His voice echoed in the stillness. "The water's great!"

I saw his clothes piled up by the steps at the shallow end. I peeled down to my underwear and tossed my clothes next to his.

I scurried up the diving-board steps and did a cannonball into the deep end. "WHOOOEEEE!" I shouted as I hit the water.

"Marco!" Connor yelled as I came up for air.

"Polo!" I shouted back. I dove underwater and swam to the other end. I felt his arm brush against me as I came up for air.

"Got ya!" he exclaimed.

I squirted a mouthful of water at him through my teeth.

"Hey, you got me right in the eye!" Connor complained.

I heard him get out of the pool and run to the diving board.

"Look out beloooooow!" he shouted.

He made a huge splash. I heard him come up for air.

"Bet that was a belly flop," I remarked.

55

But Connor was silent.

"Jack?" he asked after a minute. "I just thought of something."

"What?" I lolled on my back in the water.

"When are we supposed to get visible again?"

"Luana said it would last until sundown," I replied. "Why?"

"Look out the window," Connor told me.

I glanced out the big window to the west.

The sun was gone from the sky.

It was dark out.

And we were still invisible.

Oh, no. I suddenly felt a tightness in my chest.

What if we never turned visible again?

What if we stayed this way forever?

12

I didn't have much time to worry about becoming visible again, though.

Tapping footsteps echoed through the pool room.

"Jack," Connor whispered. "Someone's coming!"

The footsteps came closer. They sounded like someone in high heels.

"Don't move and they won't know we're here," I cautioned.

I held my breath.

A skinny woman carrying a clipboard strode into the pool area. She was talking to a big guy in coveralls.

"We think these tiles ought to be replaced," she told him. She crouched down right next to me and pointed to a group of tiles only inches away from my head.

"Yep," the man said, nodding. "They need replacing all right."

They were so close, I could smell the woman's perfume.

I had to get out of there. But how?

Then I felt a strange tingling sensation on the tips of my fingers. It traveled up my arms.

What was it?

My skin started to burn. I felt as if I were on fire.

My heart hammered in my chest. Sweat dripped down my forehead. I desperately wanted to dunk myself under the water, but I was too afraid they would hear me.

The woman stood up and walked over to the diving board. The man followed her.

I quickly sank down under the water, but it didn't help. The tingling, burning feeling got worse.

I came up for air just in time to hear the woman say "Oops! I left my pen over there."

She headed back my way.

The tingling was unbearable. I clenched my teeth to keep from screaming.

The woman stopped in her tracks. Her mouth dropped open. Her eyes grew round.

"W-what in the—" the woman stammered.

My heart thudded.

Was she staring at me?

Could she *see* me?

No, her gaze was aimed about two feet to my right.

I glanced over.

Next to me, the image of Connor's face wavered. It was like looking at a reflection in rippling water. Then it became more and more solid.

Finally, his whole head and body were visible again.

I stared down at my own hands.

I could see them!

I was visible again.

And I was in my underwear!

"Let's move!" I yelled.

Connor dashed up the pool steps and grabbed his clothes. I was right behind him.

"What are you doing here?" the woman with the clipboard shouted. "Where did you come from?"

"Hurry up!" I shouted to Connor.

I grabbed my pile of clothes and took off after Connor.

"Come back here!" the woman called. "You have some explaining to do!"

Not in my underwear, I didn't!

We tore out the back door. In the parking lot we ducked behind the white van to pull on our clothes.

I glanced around the parking lot. No one else there.

No one to see me being embarrassed yet again.

Besides the lady with the clipboard, that is. And the pool repairman. But I had a feeling they wouldn't tell anyone.

"I'm f-f-freezing!" Connor complained through chattering teeth.

"Me too!" I agreed. "Let's go home."

* * *

I made it home and got dry without anyone noticing. Even nosy Carrie didn't say anything to me. But then, Carrie didn't say much all evening. I think she was still recovering from her doll talking to her.

I didn't say much all evening either.

Something was bugging me.

It was great being invisible.

But now that the day was over, I remembered about Luana.

Luana. We had a deal with her.

She kept her bargain. She made us invisible.

Now we had to go back and help her. That was the deal.

But the thought of going back to that mausoleum sent chills up my back. Especially now—now that I knew her powers were real.

Finally I decided I had to talk to Connor about it. I took the cordless up to my room and dialed his number.

We talked about dumb stuff for a while. Then I took a deep breath and cut to the chase.

"I guess now we'll have to go back to Luana," I said. "Time to keep our half of the deal."

"Are you nuts?" Connor cried.

"But we promised," I argued.

"Jack, there's no way I'm going back. I didn't want to have anything to do with her when I thought she *didn't* have magic powers. Now that I know she *does,* I'm staying far, far away, man. I mean, she lives in a

60

tomb in the Fear Street Cemetery! What could be creepier than that?"

I knew we were in trouble if even Connor was scared.

I was definitely spooked. And I didn't want to go back to the cemetery ever again.

But what if she came after us?

I shuddered, thinking of her sad blue eyes and pale hands.

She was spooky.

Ultra spooky.

"I don't know. . . ." I murmured. I twisted my spider ring around my finger.

"Stay away from her, Jack," Connor warned. "I'm telling you, she's bad news. Besides, what could we do for her? She wants us to find her family or something, right? How can we do that? We're just kids. She needs a detective agency. Not us."

"Maybe you're right," I said at last.

I hung up and got into bed. I lay there, staring at the glow-in-the-dark star stickers on my bedroom ceiling.

Wind howled through the trees outside. The sound of it gave me the creeps. It almost sounded human.

I tried not to think of Luana. But I couldn't help it.

Were Connor and I making a mistake? Luana had these magic powers. Who knew what she could do to us if we made her mad?

The wind suddenly grew louder. My wooden shutters banged against the side of the house.

My room felt icy cold. I rolled myself up in my blankets.

Then I noticed the curtains swaying. A shiver danced on my spine.

Was there someone—something—in the room with me?

"Jaaaaack . . . Jaaaack . . ." a faint voice called.

It sounded as though it was right outside my window. As though someone was hovering there, calling to me.

The hair on the back of my neck prickled. Don't be an idiot. It's only the wind, I tried to tell myself.

"Jaaack . . ."

There it was again!

"Jaaack . . . promise . . . Jaaaaack . . ."

Could the wind say "promise"?

No way.

The voice I heard was not the wind.

It was Luana!

She was coming after me!

13

I threw off the covers and raced to my window.

I stared out into the night.

There was no one there. No pale, sad-eyed girl outside.

Just the dark backyard. Trees tossing in the wind.

I got back into bed. But I barely slept for the rest of the night. Every time I nodded off, I saw Luana's sad blue eyes and heard her voice.

Connor and I rode our bikes to school the next day. On the way there we made a pact not to tell anyone about our disappearing act. There was no way anyone would believe us.

It had to be our little secret.

I didn't tell Connor about the voice the night before. That was *my* little secret. I knew he would say

I was hearing things anyway. He would say it was my guilty conscience.

I went to the bathroom right before class. There was no one else in there. But as I was washing my hands, all the toilets started flushing.

By themselves.

Then all the faucets turned on.

Just like yesterday.

Something weird was happening. Something very weird.

Then I felt someone standing right behind me.

I glanced in the mirror.

I caught a glimpse of pale skin. Blond hair. Sad blue eyes.

It was her! Luana!

I let out a yelp and spun around.

There was no one there.

"No way," I muttered. I raced down the line of stalls, throwing the doors open.

But they were all empty. No one hiding inside and playing a trick on me.

I strolled out of the bathroom as casually as I could, but my legs still felt shaky and weak.

I walked to class in a daze.

Did I really see Luana? Or was it just my mind playing tricks on me?

I slid into my seat next to Connor just as the bell rang. I opened my knapsack and peered in, searching for a sharp pencil.

I felt someone breathing in my ear.

"Jack, come back to the cemetery," a voice whispered.

I screamed and dropped my bag on the floor. I swung around.

Connor was staring at me. "What's with you?" he demanded. "All I did was ask you if you had an extra pencil."

Ms. Beamus rapped her knuckles on her desk. "Jack! Connor!" she called sharply. "Quiet, please."

"Sorry," I mumbled. I picked up my knapsack and fished out a couple of pencils. I handed one to Connor.

Maybe he did ask me for a pencil. But that wasn't what I heard.

I heard Luana's voice.

Somehow, she was making me hear things. See things.

She was out to get me!

For the rest of the morning nothing else happened. I didn't see or hear Luana again.

Did that mean she was going to leave me alone?

I hoped so.

At lunch I took my place in line right behind Penny.

I gave her a knowing smile.

"We missed you yesterday," I told her. "Where were you?"

"What do you care?" Penny demanded.

I remembered how she looked standing on her bed

with her sheets wrapped around her. My smile grew even wider.

"What are you smiling at?" she asked suspiciously.

"Oh, nothing." I shrugged. "Nothing at all."

"Weirdo," Penny muttered.

I took a bowl of watery vegetable beef soup from the lunch lady and headed toward Connor's table.

I sat down and dipped my soup spoon into my bowl.

Something was reflecting in the soup.

I peered into my bowl, frowning.

It couldn't be.

But it was.

Right in front of my eyes, in my bowl of soup, Luana's face wavered. In the middle of the potatoes and carrots!

The hair on my arms prickled. I stirred the soup, hoping the image would fade away. But it didn't.

Her watery, pale face kept staring back at me.

"What's wrong with you?" Connor asked. "You look spooked."

I glanced up at Connor and took a few deep breaths, trying to make myself speak. But I couldn't. My lips wouldn't move.

"Jack, what's going on?" Connor demanded. "You've been acting weird all day."

I stared into the soup once more.

She was gone. She had disappeared. Again.

I decided I had to tell Connor. Maybe the same thing was happening to him. I hitched my chair closer to him.

"Weird things have been happening to me," I told him quietly.

"Huh? What kind of things?" Connor asked. He shoved a spoonful of soup in his mouth.

"Well," I began to tell him, "last night I thought I heard Luana calling to me. Then, right before first period, I could have sworn I saw her in the bathroom with me."

"The *boys'* bathroom?" Connor looked shocked.

I nodded impatiently. "Yes. But when I turned around, she was gone. And just now—" I hesitated, knowing how stupid it sounded. "Just now she was in my soup."

Connor's eyes widened. "She was in your *soup?*"

I gazed down at my plate. "I know it sounds funny—"

"Jack, listen," Connor said patiently. "You're just feeling guilty."

I scowled. "I knew you were going to say that."

"Well, it's true," Connor insisted. "I mean, how come this is all happening to you and not me? *I* haven't had any weird Luana visions. Because *I* don't feel guilty about not going back to that mausoleum. I know that girl is spooky, and I have no problem staying far, far away from her."

I decided to drop it. I knew Connor was wrong. I wasn't seeing Luana because of my guilty conscience. I was seeing her because she put some kind of spell on me.

But I didn't feel up to convincing him.

67

For the rest of the day I couldn't get my mind off Luana. Everywhere I went, I worried that I might see her. Staring at me. Beckoning to me. Calling me.

I couldn't concentrate in any of my classes. When the last bell rang, I jumped out of my desk and raced toward the door.

"What's your hurry?" Connor called. "Let's play some ball."

"Got to get home early," I said over my shoulder. "I promised my mom I'd help her clean the basement."

I hated lying to Connor, but I really needed to be alone. I had to sort this all out.

I hopped on my bike and pedaled home.

Why wasn't Luana haunting Connor? I wondered. Why was she after just me?

I turned my bike down Fear Street. All kinds of thoughts whizzed through my head as I rode along the creepy street with its run-down houses.

But it all came down to one thing.

I had to live up to my end of the bargain. Luana made me invisible. Now I had to help her. Or at least try.

I had to go back to the Fear Street Cemetery.

And if Connor wouldn't come with me, I'd do it alone.

14

I decided to go to the cemetery right away. Right this very second. If I didn't, I knew I'd lose my nerve.

I stopped my bike in front of the rusted iron gate.

The gate creaked as I pushed it open. My breath came out in white puffs in the wintry air.

I almost turned back. But I stopped myself.

My hands trembled as I locked my bike to the cemetery fence. I cautiously picked my way through the tombstones until I was standing right in front of the mausoleum.

Everything was still and cold.

"Luana?" I whispered. "Luana, are you here?"

No one responded.

Great. Now what?

I gazed at the stone carving near the door.

Was it staring back?

I brought her to life by kissing the carving. Maybe if I kissed it again . . .

I climbed the mausoleum steps slowly. I glanced around the cemetery.

Not a soul in sight.

I took a deep breath and leaned toward the stone face.

I kissed its lips.

They were hard and cold. Not warm, like they were before.

I closed my eyes. And waited.

I felt a hand grip my shoulder.

I gasped and spun around.

Luana!

"You came back," she said.

"W-well, um, yeah," I stammered, taking a step back from her. "I came back."

Luana smiled. "I knew you would."

"Uh—right." Sure she knew. She *made* me come back!

"I'm glad," Luana went on. "I still need your help."

I shrugged. "I really don't see what I can do. I mean, I'm just a kid. I'm not a sorcerer or anything—"

She put her finger to her lips. "Shhh. Let me explain."

She motioned for me to sit on the mausoleum steps. I sat down and waited for her to begin.

"Inside this mausoleum is something that is very important to me. I need it to get back to my family.

The evil sorcerer put a spell on it, so I cannot touch it. But you, Jack, can touch this thing and bring it back to me."

Her eyes narrowed as she gazed at me. I wanted to look away, but I found myself staring back at her.

I cleared my throat. "What is this thing?"

She smiled at me. It was the saddest smile I had ever seen.

"Only a tiny gold fly," she told me.

I bit my lip.

A tiny gold fly couldn't hurt me. And I did owe her. She made me invisible, just as I asked.

"I'll help you all I can," Luana added. "I will make you invisible again, in case there is any danger. But you must be quick. I can keep the spell going for only a little while. My powers are wearing thin."

I swallowed hard and nodded.

"All you need to do is to walk in, find the gold fly, and then bring it back to me," she explained. "Can you do that, Jack?"

I gaped at the mausoleum. It seemed even darker than before.

Dead people were buried in there. Who knows how many.

There were bound to be ghosts in there too.

After all, the mausoleum was in the *Fear Street Cemetery!*

But I made a promise.

I fingered my spider ring. I had a feeling I needed more than luck, though, to pull this one off.

I stood up and faced Luana. My knees knocked together.

"Okay," I agreed, heaving a sigh. "I'll do it."

Luana nodded as if she knew all along that I would. "Are you ready?" she asked.

"Yeah, I guess," I replied.

She placed her hand on my shoulder and closed her eyes.

The sky darkened. A gust of wind whipped Luana's long blond hair across her face.

She gripped my shoulder harder. I felt a surge of energy shoot through my shoulder, knocking me backward.

"W-what just happened?" I stammered. I shook my head. I felt dizzy and queasy. I rubbed my shoulder. It felt sore, as if I had just pitched for twenty innings in a row.

Luana opened her eyes and looked me up and down. "Good," she said. "Now you are prepared for anything."

I peered down at my feet, but I could no longer see them.

I was invisible again.

15

I grasped the brass handle of the mausoleum door and yanked it open.

I stepped in. The door slammed behind me.

"Good luck," I heard Luana cry from the other side.

I plastered my body flat against the door. Every muscle felt tense.

A few rays of light leaked in from the tiny window above the door. I scanned the small, dark room. It was completely bare, with a stone floor and stone walls. Big, thick cobwebs clung to every corner.

I searched in the dimness, hoping to spot the tiny gold fly. But there was nothing except a few spiders.

Across from me was a staircase leading down. Down underground.

My eyes locked on it. I knew I'd have to go down it to find the fly.

No way. No way! I thought. It's way too creepy.

But I had to do it. Or Luana would use her magic to haunt me forever!

I crept toward the staircase and looked down. It was too dark to see what was at the bottom.

I didn't want to go down there. Didn't want to see what was at the bottom of that creepy staircase.

But I promised Luana I'd bring back that dumb fly.

I tiptoed down the stone steps. My legs trembled. The lower I went, the darker it got. It smelled damp and moldy.

Once I was a few feet from the bottom, I could see that there were three tunnels leading off the landing.

"Oh, great," I groaned. An underground maze.

How was I supposed to tell which way to go?

Luana said I had to move fast. So I closed my eyes and aimed my finger blindly.

I opened my eyes. I was pointing at the middle passage.

Middle it was. I started toward it.

I could barely see anything. I felt along the wall, hoping for a light switch.

Yeah, right! In a mausoleum!

I stumbled down the passage. After a while I noticed a faint greenish glow coming from the walls.

Was it some kind of magic? Or maybe radioactive slime?

Anything was possible under the Fear Street Cemetery.

I imagined dead bodies, walking, stalking behind me.

Then—the passage abruptly ended.

Wrong way. I had to go back to where I started.

As quickly as I could, I groped my way back to the landing. This time I chose the entrance to my right. I stepped into it cautiously. I had to be careful. There could be more dead ends.

I followed the twists and turns. I came to a fork. I veered right, then followed that passage. To another fork. Right again.

Yet another fork. This one had three branches.

I chose the left one.

And then I came to *another* dead end.

Sweat dripped down my neck as I made my way back to the three-way fork.

"Which way now?" I muttered.

Just then I heard something stir in one of the other tunnels.

Was someone in here with me?

I stiffened. My fists clenched.

I stood up and took a step toward the sound. I stopped and listened again.

I heard something scraping against stone. A high-pitched screeching filled the air.

Then, in the green glow, I saw it. A squirming mass of gray fur. Hundreds of scrawny, filthy rats raced down the passage.

They were headed right for me!

I flattened myself against the wall.

I was doomed!

Any minute now they were going to chew me to pieces.

Their screeching was unbearable as they closed in on me. Needle-sharp claws tore through my socks and scraped my skin as they scurried across my feet. Scratching my ankles and calves. Running right over me in a race to find food.

Running right *over* me.

Then I remembered. They couldn't see me!

I was invisible!

I held my breath as the last rat skittered by me.

I was safe. They didn't eat me.

They didn't even know I was there!

I slumped against the wall. "That was too close," I muttered. "I'm out of here!"

Let Luana find some other idiot to do her dirty work.

I glanced to my right. Then to my left. It was so dark. Which way did I come from?

I had no idea.

My throat tightened. "Help," I croaked feebly.

But there was no one to help me.

I was alone under the Fear Street Cemetery.

And I was lost.

Totally lost.

16

"**H**ow could I be so stupid!" I groaned.

I stumbled blindly down what I thought was the way back. But after a few minutes I started to wonder if I had made a mistake.

Where were all the forks? Did I pass them in the darkness? Were they still ahead? Or was I in a different tunnel now?

I couldn't tell! It was too dark. Everything looked the same. Creepy.

Panic welled up inside me.

I whirled around and took a few steps the other way.

It was just as creepy. I thought of the hundreds of coffins in the ground above me, and shuddered.

I was lost underneath a graveyard. And there didn't seem to be any way out.

I sat down on the cold stone floor and tried to think. Maybe my sneakers left footprints. Then I could follow them back to the staircase.

I leaned down and examined the floor.

No use. I couldn't see a thing.

"I'm stuck here forever!" I bellowed.

There wasn't even an echo. The sound just died.

But then a different noise startled me. I sat up straight.

It sounded like a door opening and closing.

"Luana?" I called out.

I heard it again. I jumped up and scurried toward it.

I raced along the dark tunnel, my heart beating wildly.

Up ahead I saw something glinting. Even in the dull greenish glow, I could see it shine.

It was a huge golden door.

A golden door in the middle of nowhere?

But it made sense for the gold fly to be behind the gold door. Didn't it?

It was worth a try.

I heard something move on the other side.

"Luana?" I called again.

Still no answer.

I took a deep breath and pushed the door open.

The room on the other side seemed huge. I couldn't see the ceiling or the far wall. I crept in quietly. Darkness was all around me.

This definitely did not look like the way out.

I heard a weird sound nearby.

Something *hissed.*

Out of the corner of my eye, I thought I saw movement. I whipped around.

I could just make out two massive shapes on the other side of the room. They weren't moving though.

I clenched my teeth. I had to know what they were. Maybe they had something to do with the fly.

I crept closer to get a good look at them.

My jaw dropped. Was I dreaming?

More like a nightmare.

In front of me stood two huge bugs. Or statues of bugs.

Each of them was ten feet tall, at least.

They were made of gold.

Giant, golden *cockroaches.*

My eyes traveled up the length of their giant bodies. Over the bands on their bellies. The stiff, thick hairs on their spindly roach legs.

They were disgustingly lifelike.

I was staring straight at the huge bug on the left when I saw it.

The thing's antenna. It twitched.

Oh, no.

The roaches weren't statues.

They were alive!

17

My skin turned cold and clammy. I felt frozen to the spot.

Ten-foot-tall cockroaches? This was *worse* than my worst nightmares!

"Sssssssssssss," they hissed.

I heard spattering sounds.

The cockroaches were spitting and hissing!

"Ssssssssssssss—"

Then they began to march.

They walked on their hind legs, moving back and forth across the far end of the room. Their long, skinny feelers waved in the air. Their four front legs dangled.

It was horrible.

"Sssssssssssss—"

I hunched down a few feet away from them. I heard their spit hit the stone floor, and I tried not to shudder.

They were standing in front of something, but I couldn't make out what. I had to see what it was. What if it was the tiny gold fly? I had to grab it somehow.

I quickly glanced down at my hands.

I couldn't see them. Good. I was still invisible. That meant maybe I could sneak past the roaches.

But what if I became visible suddenly? Luana told me I didn't have much time.

Silently, I crept over to the giant bugs.

"Sssssssssssssss—" They hissed and marched. Hissed and marched.

Behind them was another door.

Click! Click! Now I could hear the faint tapping sound of their insect feet on the stone floor.

I waited until both roaches were far from the door. Then I darted between them. Carefully, I tried the door.

It was unlocked! I opened it and slipped inside.

In the middle of a small, dark room sat a fly.

It was gold.

But it wasn't tiny.

It was an *enormous* gold fly.

Bigger than the cockroaches. Bigger than a full-grown elephant. So big its wings touched the walls on either side of it.

Was *this* the "tiny" fly Luana wanted me to bring to her?

If so, it grew a lot since the last time she saw it!

The fly rubbed its furry front legs together, then it ran them over its bulging, shiny eyes. The veins in its thin gold wings pulsed as glittery fluids flowed through them.

Thick drool dripped from its jaws—jaws big enough to snap me in half. I could see a puddle of steaming saliva on the floor.

Did Luana really think I could tackle this thing? There was no way I could bring this monster to her.

Not in a million years.

I took one step backward, keeping my eyes on the drooling creature. If it knew I was there, I'd be history.

I took another slow step backward.

Just then my face felt hot. Hot and tingly.

The feeling spread down my back and across my arms.

It was as if my skin were on fire!

Then I remembered the last time I felt this way. I was in the community pool.

And I was becoming visible again.

I stared down at my hands. They were filmy, like a ghost's.

My invisibility was wearing off!

The fly's eyes rolled in its head, then fixated on me. It clicked its jaws together.

It saw me!
The fly's wings quivered.
Drool poured out of its mouth.
It was hungry.
And it was going to have me for dinner.

18

The fly crawled toward me on its skinny gold legs. Its jaws snapped open and shut, open and shut.

I crouched down on the floor, trying to make myself small. My heart beat like a jackhammer.

Maybe I could throw something at it. Like a nice fat rock.

My eyes darted around, looking for something to throw. I spotted a loose rock the size of a baseball.

Bingo!

I grabbed the rock and hurled it as hard as I could. My aim was perfect. The rock hit the fly on its bulging right eye.

The fly flinched and took a step back.

Then it advanced on me again.

The rock was too small. I needed a boulder to stop it.

Sweat poured down my back. What could I do?

The fly was barely a foot away. I felt its hot, smelly fly breath on my face. Its thick drool puddled around my feet.

Its jaws snapped open and shut. Open and shut.

The door was too far away. I'd never get there in time. I crouched as low to the floor as I could.

The fly leaned in. All I could hear was the clicking of its jaws. I held my arms up to protect my face from its huge jaws. I squeezed my eyes shut.

"Noooooo!" I screamed.

But nothing happened.

The fly didn't touch me.

Why wasn't it eating me?

I opened my eyes. The fly was backing away. As if it were afraid of me!

Its eyes rolled in its head. Its jaws clicked open and shut in a frenzy.

What was it afraid of?

I suddenly felt my ring finger throbbing. I brought my hand down to examine it.

I gaped at my spider ring.

It was glowing! Glowing with a blue light that grew brighter and brighter.

And as it grew brighter, the fly backed farther away.

I raised my hand and shone the ring's light into the fly's eyes. It stopped moving. Its wings drooped.

It looked hypnotized.

I always believed my spider ring was lucky. But I never knew it had special powers.

"Cool!" I muttered. I couldn't wait to tell Connor about this!

But first I had to get out of the fly's lair. Alive.

I tried to take a step backward.

My legs wouldn't move.

"No!" I whispered in horror. What was wrong? Did the fly's breath paralyze me or something?

Then I felt the skin tighten on my legs and arms. I heard cracking, popping sounds as my skin and bones stretched and lengthened.

This had to be magic.

But I was already visible again. What was happening to me now?

Thick, wiry black hairs sprouted on my hands and arms. Then they spread to my legs.

I could feel the skin along my ribs trembling. Then four long, skinny tendrils popped out of my sides. They lengthened and thickened. Wiggled and squirmed.

Ugh! I stared at them in horror.

What were they?

What was happening to me?

19

I stared at the wriggling black tendrils that came out of my body.

They were covered with coarse black hairs. Just like the hairs on my arms and legs. And they were jointed.

The things coming out of my side were . . . legs!

Four new legs. Plus my own arms and legs.

That made eight limbs altogether.

A scream rose in my throat. My stomach felt queasy.

I had turned into a giant spider!

The ring. My lucky spider ring. It did this to me!

Just then the fly stirred. Its gold wings trembled.

It was awakening. It rubbed its skinny gold legs together quickly, hot drool dripping from its jaws.

The fly lunged. It sank its jaws into my shoulder. Its pincers pierced my skin.

"Aaaaaah!" I screamed. Or tried to scream. But no sound came out of my spider mouth.

Stars exploded in front of my eyes. Sharp daggers of pain shot up my arm and shoulder. The fly dug its pincers in deeper and deeper. It gnawed on my shoulder.

Hot drool soaked the fur on my legs. The fly hummed with delight.

I felt dizzy and weak. Tired.

It was no use. It was eating me alive.

But I wouldn't go without a fight!

I shoved at the giant fly with my eight legs.

As I touched its quivering body, I felt a wild sensation grip me.

Wait a second. I was a spider now!

A huge, powerful spider.

Spiders *eat* flies!

Suddenly my spider instincts took over. I flexed my powerful legs. I lunged toward it, my jaws ready to bite.

The fly leaped straight up, buzzing loudly. It hovered above me, beating its wings against me, knocking me flat. Then it dove on top of me. It slapped me again and again with its strong wings.

The fly buzzed louder and louder. I got up slowly. My legs felt wobbly and weak, but I managed to reach up and sweep one across the fly's body. It fell with a thud to the ground.

88

I crawled over to it. I lunged. My jaws pierced its back.

It twisted and jerked, trying to free itself. I gripped it harder with my jaws.

The fly shuddered weakly. Finally it went limp.

I had paralyzed it!

My muscles relaxed. I slumped down onto the floor, my legs still resting on the fly's body.

Then I felt something shift under me.

Was the fly coming back to life?

I tensed my body, ready.

But the movement I felt was the fly shrinking.

It got smaller and smaller. And as it shrank, my arms and legs did too. I felt the muscles contract as they shrank back to normal. My skin loosened, then tightened again to fit snugly around my bones and muscles.

My stomach lurched queasily as my extra legs slithered back into my body. The long black hairs itched as they sank into my skin.

I rubbed my arms with the palms of my hands. The coarse hairs were completely gone.

I touched my body. The extra legs were gone too.

I was a kid again!

I peered down at the golden fly. It was the size of a normal housefly. I picked it up with my thumb and forefinger.

"That's what you get for messing with me!" I growled at the tiny insect.

89

I slipped the fly into my pocket. Now all I needed to do was to get back to Luana and give her the fly.

After what I just went through, that sounded so easy!

I twisted my ring as I thought of what to do next.

I had to get by those cockroaches again. But how could I do it now that I was visible?

I took a deep breath. I dreaded the thought of them seeing me. But I had to get out.

I crept over to the door. As silently as I could, I inched it open and peeked out.

The cockroaches crouched with their backs to me.

I crept out the door and quietly closed it.

I crouched against the wall, ready to make a break for it.

But before I could move, the cockroaches turned.

They saw me!

They hissed as they scurried toward me. Their long feelers wiggled excitedly.

I ran.

The cockroaches ran behind me. And they were fast!

The only way out was through the other gold door across the room.

But the roaches were faster. They were gaining on me.

I'd never make it!

20

My mind whirled. My heart beat double time.

Then I thought of something.

My spider ring!

It was my only hope.

I twisted the ring around my finger as I ran. "Come on, ring, do your thing!" I croaked hoarsely.

Then I turned, raised my hand, and pointed the ring at the bigger cockroach.

I held my breath and waited for the ring to glow.

Nothing happened. Not even a glimmer.

I shook my hand.

"Come on!" I yelled. "Hypnotize them! Do something!"

The cockroaches rushed toward me, hissing.

I stood frozen like a statue. Then I shook my hand again frantically.

"Please, please, please," I chanted.

But the ring still didn't change. Didn't glow. Didn't throb.

I glanced quickly from right to left. The door was so far away. I'd never make it. Never in a million years.

My eyes scanned the shadowy corners of the room. Was there someplace to hide?

I raced to another corner of the small room. But this seemed only to excite the huge cockroaches even more.

They couldn't wait to chomp on me.

I heard their spindly legs scrape across the stone floor. Their hissing filled me with dread.

"Luana!" I screamed. "Help me!"

But she couldn't hear me. I was underground.

I'd never get out of here. Never.

I was doomed!

21

I stared pleadingly at my spider ring. "Come on, come on," I begged.

No blue glow. Nothing. It was totally worthless. Whatever kind of weird magic it had was gone.

Nothing could help me now.

"Sssssssssssss—"

The larger cockroach lunged at me. Its feelers brushed against my face.

I brought my foot back and gave it a fierce kick.

Whack! My kick hit it square on its spindly front leg. I heard it go *snap*! The cockroach howled. A jet of smelly black slime spurted from its leg—right into my face.

The slimy stuff stung my eyes. It oozed down my cheeks. The stink made me gag and cough.

I raised both hands and scrubbed at my face. I had to get the slime off!

In that split second, the smaller cockroach reached for me with its hairy legs.

But I was too quick for it.

"Yaaah!" I yelled, and stomped on its front leg as hard as I could.

Crunch!

It fell on its back, then screeched in pain.

"Take that!" I hollered as I stomped on its other legs. Black slime gushed everywhere.

"That will teach you not to sneak up on me!" I screamed.

The larger cockroach limped toward me. Its feelers waved weakly. I grabbed one and yanked on it. Hard.

The feeler snapped off in my hand. It felt scaly, like a snake. And it was still quivering.

I dropped it. Yuck!

The larger cockroach lay on its side, squirming in pain. But it wasn't dead yet. It still tried to knock me over with one of its legs.

"Fat chance, roach-face!" I shouted.

I was mad now. Madder than I'd ever been in my life.

I was done being scared.

I ran straight into the roach and kicked it in the belly with every last bit of strength I had.

The larger cockroach curled itself up into a tight little ball. The smaller one was making a few feeble attempts to right itself.

"I am out of here!" I yelled.

I patted my jacket, making sure the fly was still there. I'd be able to keep my promise to Luana.

I hurried to the door, opened it, then slammed it behind me.

The cockroaches were down for now, but what if they recovered?

Then I'd *really* be in trouble.

"I better hurry," I muttered.

I ran down the tunnel until I reached the three-way fork.

Which one? I tried to remember how I got here in the first place.

I stepped to the right and hurried forward. At a fork, I turned left. Then left again.

I just hoped I was going the right way!

I pumped my legs. Faster. Faster. Those cockroaches might not be down for long.

And then—

I strained my eyes to peer ahead of me. Was that a beam of light up there? Real, natural light?

"The staircase?" I whispered.

My legs felt rubbery and weak. I gasped for breath.

I kept my hand in my jacket pocket as I raced along the passage. I couldn't afford to lose the gold fly now. Not when I was so close.

Nothing could stop me now!

And then I was covering the final few yards to the staircase. I gathered my strength to spring up the steps.

And felt something jump on my leg.

I glanced down. A huge gray rat clung to my jeans. Hanging by its teeth.

"Get off!" I screamed, shaking my leg.

But the rat hung on. Squeaking fiercely. Scratching with its hind legs.

"Get off!" I repeated.

I shook my leg harder.

The rat flew off and hit the wall with a thud.

I leaped up the stairs two at a time. Dashed across the small room and yanked the door open.

"Luana!" I called. "Luana! I'm back!"

I slumped against the stone door, trying to catch my breath. There was no moon out, so it was dark. So dark, I could barely see anything. A cold breeze blew, sending shivers up my back.

"Luana?" I called again. "Are you here?"

Someone grabbed my shoulder. I spun around.

"Did you get it?" Luana asked eagerly. "Did you get the gold fly?"

I felt my cheeks turn hot. After everything I had been through, all she cared about was her lousy fly!

I bit my lip to keep from screaming at her.

"Yes, I got your stupid fly," I said through clenched teeth. "But you tricked me! Why didn't you tell me the truth? That was no 'tiny little fly.' It was huge. I almost got killed in there!"

Luana just nodded. "Good," she murmured. "You've done well. Now give me the fly."

I was so annoyed, I felt tempted to tell her to go jump in a lake. But then I remembered her magic powers.

I didn't want to make Luana mad at me.

I reached into my pocket and pulled the fly out. I took one last, long look at it before handing it to her. It had been tough. But I did it! I kept my promise.

Now I could go on with my life.

"Thank you," Luana said. She peered at the fly closely.

Then she tossed it into the woods.

"Hey!" I cried. I leaped down the mausoleum steps. "What are you doing? I thought you needed that! I thought you—"

"I don't need it," Luana replied calmly.

"What do you mean?" I stared at her. "Why did you put me through all that then?"

"I don't need the fly," Luana repeated. "I just needed you to use up all the power in your ring."

My mind spun.

How did she know about the power in my ring?

"What are you talking about?" I demanded.

"That obstacle course in there—it was for you to use up the power in your ring. You really don't remember who you are?" Luana asked.

"Of course I know who I am," I said. "I'm Jack Meyers."

Luana shook her head. "No," she said simply. "You're not. You are Jacobus."

"Jacobus?" I echoed. A panic rose in my chest. "What in the world are you talking about?"

Luana stared into my eyes. A slow smile curved her lips.

"You are Jacobus," she repeated. "The sorcerer's son."

22

I shook my head slowly, backing away from her.

"You're nuts," I declared. "Totally crazy. My name is Jack Meyers. Ask anyone."

"I see you don't believe me," Luana said. "Let me explain."

"Go ahead," I replied. "But I still won't believe you."

Luana narrowed her eyes at me. "You were always envious of me, Jacobus. Always. I risked your father's anger to read his books. I learned the spells by myself, late at night. But you"— Luana pointed her long, skinny finger at me—"you were too busy riding your fancy horses and eating your fancy meals. And so you never learned a single spell. Not one!" Her face flushed with anger as she spat the words out.

"When your father caught me in his library, he

worried about my powers," Luana continued. "He didn't know how much I had learned from his books, so he imprisoned me in this tomb. You followed me, Jacobus."

Jacobus. Jacobus. She kept repeating that weird name.

Something about it stirred memories in the back of my mind. Weird memories.

Suddenly I saw a room filled with dusty old books. A tall man with a pointy gray beard poring over them. And a girl with sad blue eyes.

Luana.

I shook my head.

"It isn't true!" I murmured. "It isn't!"

"You were so evil," Luana told me. "You once locked me in a closet for three days simply because I said hello to you. And there were days when you insisted that I was to be fed only bread crusts. It was because you knew I had talent. And that you would never be as good a sorcerer as I."

Memories swirled around in my head. I saw Luana in a small dark room, begging to be let out. I saw her eating bread crusts and staring silently at me.

But she had been rude! How dare she even speak to me!

It was all coming back to me now. Her rudeness. Her nerve. She got what she deserved!

I clenched my fists, waiting for her to continue her silly story.

"When your father sent me to this tomb," Luana

said, "he wanted you to be safe. So he put you in a different time. A different form. And in case I ever escaped my prison and found you again, he gave you the ring. It might have defeated me. But its magic, though very powerful, is limited. The spells in my head are forever."

I gazed down at my ring. The magic was all gone. And it was her fault!

A slight smile crossed Luana's face. "You lost all memory when you traveled in time. You forgot everything, even the power of the ring. So you lived for years as Jack Meyers on Fear Street. Never knowing that your name, your family—your entire life—was just an illusion! Never knowing your true identity—as Jacobus, son of the most powerful sorcerer on earth!"

She laughed.

The sound of it filled me with rage. How dare she laugh at me!

"I knew my one hope was to draw you to me. And you were so easy to find! The ring sent out a signal to me," Luana said. "Then all I had to do was get you to use up all its power. And that, too, was easy."

More and more memories. Of looking into a mirror and seeing another boy. Not short, skinny Jack Meyers—though the face was very similar. But this boy was brutal. Muscular. Tall. And his eyes were full of anger.

My body started to tremble. A powerful rush of energy surged through my veins.

I gazed at my hands.

They were suddenly bigger. Stronger.

I ran my fingers through my hair. It was curlier.

My muscles bulged against my shirt. The skin on my legs burned as my legs lengthened and grew thicker.

I felt myself being pulled up as my entire body grew.

I was at least a foot taller!

I *was* Jacobus! Son of Arlin!

And I would not, could not, let this peasant do this to me!

Luana looked me up and down and shook her head sadly. "You are back to your true body, Jacobus. But I am free now. Free to live the life your father took away from me."

Her eyes had a faraway look in them. As if she were already there, sitting by the fire with her family.

She couldn't do this to me! I was Jacobus!

"This will never work." I sneered at her. "The power of the ring will return. And then I will find you and make you pay!"

Luana frowned. "That's what you think, Jacobus!" she snapped. A cold, hard expression crept across her face.

Luana opened the mausoleum door.

What did she think she was doing? She was still such a stupid, rude girl!

"Don't open that door!" I demanded. "Something might get out!"

"Or something might get in!" she cried.

And she pushed me!

Me! Jacobus!

She was small. Thin. Weak. But she caught me off guard.

I stumbled backward.

Into the tomb.

"See you in a century or so!" Luana cried.

And slammed the mausoleum door in my face.

I was trapped inside.

Forever.

23

"Luana!" I shouted. I beat against the stone door of the mausoleum. "Don't do this to me! I'm sorry! I won't punish you! You must save me!"

Then I heard the sound I was dreading.

Hissing.

The cockroaches!

The hissing came from below. They must have heard me. And now they were crawling up the steps.

"Luana," I called again. "The cockroaches! Save me from them! They'll eat me alive!"

I couldn't hear anything on the other side of the door.

Did she leave me here? Leave me to be eaten alive?

How could she do that to me! I was Jacobus, son of Arlin!

"I'll protect you from them, Jacobus." Luana's

voice came faintly through the door. "In thanks for taking my place."

"Taking your place! No! You can't! Listen to me, Luana!"

I pounded the door with my fists.

"Farewell, Jacobus!" Luana called.

I pounded the door again. Harder.

She had to come back! She had to!

"You said you'd save me from the cockroaches!" I yelled.

No answer.

"Luana!"

Still no answer.

"I'll get you for this, Luana!" I screamed at her. "You'll see! Just you wait!"

But my voice sounded strangely hoarse all of a sudden.

And I could barely breathe.

My throat felt clogged, as if someone had stuffed a sock into it.

I couldn't move my arms. I couldn't move my legs. It was as if they had turned to stone.

I felt so heavy. So very, very heavy . . .

24

"Hey, Brittany, let's cut through the Fear Street Cemetery!" Penny Morris cried.

Brittany Carson wrinkled up her nose. "Yuck. It's creepy in there!"

Penny grabbed Brittany's parka. "Come on, don't be dumb. There's no such thing as ghosts."

Brittany rolled her eyes. "Oh, okay. But let's hurry."

She followed Penny through the rusted iron cemetery gate.

Inside, Brittany pulled up the hood of her parka. "It seems colder here," she murmured. "Weird."

"It's just your imagination. Come on," Penny urged.

In the center of the cemetery Brittany spotted a weird house. A house made of stone.

"What's that?" she asked, pointing.

"It's a mausoleum. Cool!" Penny declared. "Let's check it out."

She raced up the stone steps.

Brittany lingered behind. "Come on, Penny," she complained. "This place is creepy. And I want to get to Randi's house. What if they start watching the video without us?"

Penny waved her hand impatiently. "In a second. You've got to see this!" she cried. "It's too weird!"

"What is it?" Brittany asked, narrowing her eyes.

"It's a face carved into a stone," Penny whispered.

"Huh?" Brittany asked. She crept up the mausoleum steps to see what Penny was staring at.

The face of a boy was carved into the stone door. A boy with curly hair and fierce, angry eyes.

Brittany stared. It reminded her of someone. But who?

Penny poked the carved face. "He looks kind of like that kid, Jack Meyers, who used to go to school with us. You know. The one who disappeared—with his whole family."

Brittany shivered. "That was so weird. I wonder what happened to them."

"I heard they left their clothes and furniture and everything," Penny commented. "Maybe they were running from the law or something!"

"Maybe," Brittany agreed.

"Hey, look!" Penny exclaimed. "There's a poem written here. Listen to this:

"For years and years
I've lived in stone
But you can set me free.
Kiss my lips
To bring me back
That is my only plea."

Brittany sighed. "Wow. That's kind of . . . romantic."

"Go ahead, then," Penny said, laughing. "Kiss the statue."

"Me? Why should *I* do it?" Brittany demanded.

Penny smirked. "Well, it does kind of look like Jack. And you kind of liked him—even though he was a total loser."

Brittany's cheeks turned red. "I did not."

She stared at the carved face.

"Go on," Penny urged. "Kiss it."

Brittany leaned forward.

Then she jerked back with a laugh.

"No way. This is too dumb."

"Oh, come on." Penny sounded disappointed.

"No." Brittany shook her head and started down the steps. "Let's just go. It's getting late. . . ."

Are you ready for another walk
down Fear Street?
Turn the page for a terrifying
sneak preview.

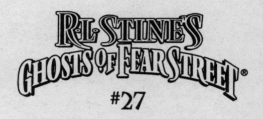

#27

PARENTS FROM THE
13TH DIMENSION

Coming mid-November 1997

I opened my eyes to bright sunlight.

I sat straight up. Did I fall asleep? I must have. Did I sleep all the way through to Friday morning?

What time was it, anyway? Was I late for school?

I swung my foot over the edge of my bed. But it touched only air. I stared down at the floor. Why did it seem so far away?

Then I glanced at my leg. I had on pajamas.

Pajamas? When did I take off my jeans?

And—hey! These weren't *my* pajamas! Mine were old red plaid flannel ones that Hal outgrew. These were nice white cotton ones.

Whose pajamas was I wearing?

And . . . wait a minute! My eyes grew wide as I gazed around the room.

It looked like my room. Sort of. The door was in the same place. The window, too. It had the same wide window seat. The same old oak tree stood right outside the window.

But now white curtains fluttered in the breeze. On the walls was delicate flowered wallpaper.

And I was sitting on a bed. A *real* bed! It was high up off the floor. It had a white wicker headboard. And nice clean sheets! And instead of a ratty old blanket woven by my dad, there was a white feather comforter.

"What a great dream!" I murmured. "If only it was real!"

I closed my eyes and opened them again.

Everything was still there. The wicker bed. The flowered wallpaper. The billowing curtains.

My heart began to pound in my chest.

The room was great. But if I wasn't dreaming, then . . .

Where was I?

My head whirled as I crossed to the dressing table by the window. It had a big mirror. I stared into it.

I half expected to see a strange face staring back at me. But I didn't. I saw my same round face. My same large brown eyes and wide mouth. My same blond hair.

What was going on?

Quietly I opened the door to my room—or whos-ever room it was—and tiptoed into the hallway.

It was like the hallway outside my room. Except

that it was freshly painted and not full of dust bunnies.

My bare feet didn't make a sound on the thick blue carpet as I ran down the stairs.

I stopped outside the kitchen. I heard muffled voices. But whose voices were they? I didn't recognize them.

What happened to Mom, Dad, and Hal?

I took a few steps into the kitchen.

It looked like my old kitchen—but shiny copper pots hung over the stove. A big silvery refrigerator gleamed. Everything was new and clean and expensive looking.

A woman stood at the stove, her back to me. A woman in a silky green dress and high heels. Over the dress she wore an apron. It was tied in the back with a bow.

That *definitely* wasn't my mom!

A man and a teenage boy sat at a table by the window. The man had on a dark blue business suit and a striped tie. His hair was slicked back. He wore small wire-rimmed glasses and he was reading *The Wall Street Journal.*

The boy appeared to be about fourteen. My brother Hal's age. But this boy was no nerd. He had sun-bleached blond hair. He looked like a movie actor! He was reading the back of a cereal box.

No one noticed me standing there. I didn't make a sound.

Then I saw what was under the table. A dog! An adorable yellow dog! A Labrador, maybe, with floppy ears and big brown eyes. It was hardly more than a puppy.

I couldn't help myself. I gasped.

The man lowered his newspaper. The boy looked up from the cereal box. The woman turned around from the stove.

All I could do was stare at them.

A million thoughts flashed through my mind.

They would demand to know who I was. And what I was doing in their house.

What could I tell them? Would they call the police? Could I end up in jail?

What were they going to do?

And then they all broke into big smiles.

The man spoke first.

"Good morning, Sarah!" he said cheerfully. "How's my favorite daughter today?"

Daughter?

"Excuse me?" I managed.

"I said, 'Good morning!'" The man smiled.

"Sit down, sweetheart," the woman told me. "Your French toast is almost ready."

I didn't know these people. They were complete strangers!

Yet *they* seemed to know *me*. What was going on?

My stomach growled again. In a daze, I walked to the table. The dog scooted out from under it. It jumped up on me, licking my hand and yapping.

"Sparky's ready for his walk," the boy said. He stood up. "I'll take him for you, Sarah. Go ahead and eat your breakfast."

"Okay," I muttered, sitting down shakily at the table.

"That's nice of you, Jason," the woman declared.

She walked over to the table. I caught a scent of her flowery perfume. It smelled wonderful. She put a plate of hot French toast down in front of me. Butter was melting on top. Beside the toast were strips of bacon. It looked so good!

The man passed me a jug of syrup. "Eat up, Sarah," he said.

I was hungry. But I was scared to eat. What if it was some kind of trick? I didn't have a clue who these people were. Or how they knew my name. Or what they wanted from me.

The man and woman kept smiling at me. I didn't know what to do. So I picked up my fork. The woman nodded encouragingly.

I took a bite. But I was too upset to taste my food.

How could these people think I was their daughter? Who were they? How did I get into their house? Was I dreaming?

Was I going crazy?

All I could think of was to go along with these strangers. And hope I could figure out what was happening.

Jason came back with Sparky as I finished my breakfast. The dog jumped on my chair, begging. I slipped him some bacon.

"Sarah!" the woman said with a laugh. "You know better than to give Sparky table food. It's for you, sweetheart."

I drew my hand away. "Sorry, Sparky," I murmured.

"Hurry and get dressed if you want to walk to school with me, Sarah," Jason said.

"Oh, um—okay," I mumbled.

I thanked the woman for breakfast and headed for the stairs. On the way, I glanced into the living room. My jaw dropped.

Over the fireplace hung a large portrait. A family portrait of the man, the woman, Jason and . . . and *me!*

I swallowed. I walked slowly closer to the portrait. It smelled faintly of oil paint. I stared.

There I was—or, at least, there was a girl who looked exactly like me. Sitting between the man and Jason. Sitting at a table spread with what looked like Christmas dinner.

How did I get into this picture?

The million unanswered questions plus the paint smell made me dizzy. I pulled myself away from the portrait. I ran back up to "my room." I wanted to lie down on the bed.

I needed to think!

"Sarah," Jason called. "Hurry up! We'll be late."

No time to think. I just had to keep playing along for now.

*   *   *

As we walked to school, Jason talked. I listened, hoping he might drop a clue. A clue that would let me in on the big secret that everybody but me seemed to know.

But all he talked about was his phone. How it wasn't working. How his friend Brian might call him on my line.

My line! I had my own phone *and* my own line!

This dream world—or whatever it was—was so cool!

A round-faced girl with brown hair ran up to us as we reached the corner.

"Hey, Sarah!" she called. "How's it going, Jason?"

"Hey, Zoe," Jason said. "Well, this is where I turn off. Bye, Zoe. I'll see you later, Sarah."

Zoe walked the rest of the way to school with me. Like Jason, she seemed to have known me forever. Too weird!

We reached a building that looked like a brand-new Shadyside Middle School. Letters carved over its front door spelled out Sunnyside Middle School.

*Sunny*side?

I followed Zoe to her locker. She twirled the dial.

"Aren't you going to hang up your coat, Sarah?" she asked.

"Um, I forgot my locker combination," I muttered.

Zoe reached over and opened the locker next to hers. "Like you ever lock it," she said with a laugh.

I stuffed my coat inside and shut the locker.

Zoe shouldered her bookbag. "So what's your brother doing this weekend?"

"Hal?" I shrugged. "Probably sitting at the computer and—"

"Hal?" Zoe cut me off. "Hello, Sarah! Your brother's name is Jason." She gave me an odd look. "Do you feel okay?"

"Yeah," I said quickly. "I'm fine. Really."

And I was!

Maybe I didn't know what was going on. Maybe this was all a dream. Maybe soon I'd wake up and it would be over.

But as long as it lasted, I was going to enjoy every single minute of my amazing dream!

At dinnertime the dream was still going strong. Which was great, because I wouldn't have wanted to miss that dinner. Pot roast—yum! And chocolate sundaes for dessert.

The woman in the green dress might not be my real mom. But she could cook a thousand times better than my real mom!

Afterward we all played Monopoly. At first I had trouble calling the woman and man "Mother" and "Father." But as we played, I got used to it. I liked it, in fact. It made me feel sort of classy.

Before I went up to bed, Jason said something about going to the stables first thing in the morning.

The stables! I could hardly wait!

I wrote about my incredible day in my diary. Then

I crawled into bed, happy and full. I fell asleep right away.

But in the middle of the night, I heard a noise. I sat up.

There it was again. A low sound. Like something ripping.

I climbed out of bed and opened my door. The noise grew louder. It was a noise I knew. But what?

Then I had it! Someone was pulling apart strips of Velcro.

I stepped out into the hallway.

The ripping sound came from behind a closed door at the end of the hall. In my *real* house, a storage room was behind that door.

But what was behind it in this house?

I tiptoed toward the door.

I reached for the knob. It turned easily.

The door clicked open.

Then an icy claw clutched my shoulder. It dug into my flesh.

And a terrible, hissing voice said, "Sssarah—ssssstop!"

About R.L. Stine

R.L. Stine is the best-selling author in America. He has written more than one hundred scary books for young people, all of them best-sellers.

His series include *Fear Street, Ghosts of Fear Street* and the *Fear Street Sagas*.

Bob grew up in Columbus, Ohio. Today he lives in New York City with his wife, Jane, his teenage son, Matt, and his dog, Nadine.

R.L. STINE'S
GHOSTS OF FEAR STREET ®

1 HIDE AND SHRIEK	52941-2/$3.99
2 WHO'S BEEN SLEEPING IN MY GRAVE?	52942-0/$3.99
3 THE ATTACK OF THE AQUA APES	52943-9/$3.99
4 NIGHTMARE IN 3-D	52944-7/$3.99
5 STAY AWAY FROM THE TREE HOUSE	52945-5/$3.99
6 EYE OF THE FORTUNETELLER	52946-3/$3.99
7 FRIGHT KNIGHT	52947-1/$3.99
8 THE OOZE	52948-X/$3.99
9 REVENGE OF THE SHADOW PEOPLE	52949-8/$3.99
10 THE BUGMAN LIVES!	52950-1/$3.99
11 THE BOY WHO ATE FEAR STREET	00183-3/$3.99
12 NIGHT OF THE WERECAT	00184-1/$3.99
13 HOW TO BE A VAMPIRE	00185-X/$3.99
14 BODY SWITCHERS FROM OUTER SPACE	00186-8/$3.99
15 FRIGHT CHRISTMAS	00187-6/$3.99
16 DON'T EVER GET SICK AT GRANNY'S	00188-4/$3.99
17 HOUSE OF A THOUSAND SCREAMS	00190-6/$3.99
18 CAMP FEAR GHOULS	00191-4/$3.99
19 THREE EVIL WISHES	00189-2/$3.99
20 SPELL OF THE SCREAMING JOKERS	00192-2/$3.99
21 THE CREATURE FROM CLUB LAGOONA	00850-1/$3.99
22 FIELD OF SCREAMS	00851-X/$3.99
23 WHY I'M NOT AFRAID OF GHOSTS	00852-8/$3.99
24 MONSTER DOG	00853-6/$3.99
25 HALLOWEEN BUGS ME	00854-4/$3.99
26 GO YOUR TOMB -- RIGHT NOW!	00855-2/$3.99

Available from Minstrel® Books
Published by Pocket Books

POCKET
B O O K S

Simon & Schuster Mail Order Dept. BWB
200 Old Tappan Rd., Old Tappan, N.J. 07675

Please send me the books I have checked above. I am enclosing $_____ (please add $0.75 to cover the postage and handling for each order. Please add appropriate sales tax). Send check or money order--no cash or C.O.D.'s please. Allow up to six weeks for delivery. For purchase over $10.00 you may use VISA: card number, expiration date and customer signature must be included.

Name _____

Address _____

City _____ State/Zip _____

VISA Card # _____ Exp.Date _____

Signature _____ 1146-24

Is The Roller Coaster Really Haunted?

THE BEAST

❑ 88055-1/$3.99

It Was An Awsome Ride—Through Time!

THE BEAST 2

❑ 52951-X/$3.99

Published by Pocket Books

Simon & Schuster Mail Order Dept. BWB
200 Old Tappan Rd., Old Tappan, N.J. 07675

Please send me the books I have checked above. I am enclosing $_____(please add $0.75 to cover the postage and handling for each order. Please add appropriate sales tax). Send check or money order--no cash or C.O.D.'s please. Allow up to six weeks for delivery. For purchase over $10.00 you may use VISA: card number, expiration date and customer signature must be included.

Name _____
Address _____
City _____ State/Zip _____
VISA Card # _____ Exp.Date _____
Signature _____ 1163